"It is a pity you have not a more suitable set of friends, for young gentlemen of moderate means could ill afford to keep the pace you set, I think."

"Oh I am not such an expensive fellow as all that," he laughed. "A little racing, a little sport. We find an hour now and then to attend to business. I am not about to ruin them, if that is what you fear."

"It can hardly amount to fear, as I am so little involved, but the ineligibility of yourself being used as their pattern card does cause a question."

He leveled a playful but pointed look at her. "Have you a more suitable companion in mind for me, ma'am?"

Cecilia swallowed a little gush of pleasure at this hint of wishing to spend more time with her. "I hardly know all the local inhabitants yet," her mouth said, but her eyes, which she managed with the skill of a courtesan, gave the answer he desired.

COUSIN CECILIA

Joan Smith

FAWCETT CREST • NEW YORK

A Fawcett Crest Book
Published by Ballantine Books
Copyright © 1990 by Joan Smith

Library of Congress Catalog Card Number: 90-93040

ISBN 0-449-21785-X

Manufactured in the United States of America

First Edition: September 1990

Chapter One

"THAT WAS A LOVELY DRIVE, MRS. MEACHAM," THE vicar's wife said. She put aside her well-worn pelisse and headed automatically for her favorite seat. It was one of two comfortably upholstered armchairs strategically placed in the bay window of Mrs. Meacham's saloon, to give the ladies a view of the High Street beyond. "So enjoyable to get into the countryside, especially in spring, with all the lovely greenery," she added, glancing at an indifferent chestnut tree on the corner. It would not do for the vicar's wife to admit her real interest in the view was to monitor the comings and goings of her neighbors.

"Lovely," Mrs. Meacham agreed, but with a noticeable lack of conviction. Chalk downs and sheep and trees were well enough in their way. She had had enough of them when Henry was alive, and made no bones about preferring the bustling High Street of Laycombe. The downward pull of her lips did not indicate regret at having sold one of the finest sheep farms in East Sussex and buying in its stead a mansion in the village. What did a widow, with two daughters to find husbands for, want with a great, drafty hall in the country that required a

1

bailiff and gardeners and grooms and rafts of servants? Here she and the girls were snug as fleas in a rug, at a quarter of the expense and none of the inconvenience.

"Especially in spring, with the skylarks singing," Mrs. Daugherty added, and smiled her quiet, sad smile. No matter how heavy her heart, the wife of the vicar must be patient and try to spread good will.

"Aye, but I hoped we would have more to do this spring than drive in the country." A piercing eye dared the vicar's wife to find consolation in the present situation.

Tea was brought in, and while she accepted her cup, Mrs. Daugherty gamely took up the challenge. "Perhaps he will go to London for the Season," she suggested hopefully.

"I wish he would go back to Turkey, or Greece, or wherever it is he has been racketing about the past three years."

"His influence has not been what we hoped, but surely it is better for him to be amongst Christians," Mrs. Daugherty suggested, but in no certain way. It was hard to denigrate a noble parishioner, even if he never showed his nose in church.

Mrs. Meacham sniffed and stirred three spoonfuls of sugar into her tea. She was an outspoken lady; large, dark complexioned, in a gown decorated with many embellishments. Mrs. Daugherty would look inconspicuous in any room. Next to her companion, she fairly faded away.

"The pity of it is that he is turning all our Christian young gentlemen into heathens," Mrs. Meacham declared angrily. "Henley Dallan was certainly on the verge of offering for Martha before he came along. She might have had him for the taking last year, except for her papa's passing away. Her papa favored the match. Dallan's carcass was in our saloon seven nights a week I promise you. I made sure he would make an offer on her twentieth birthday. He is no great prize, but he has that farm his uncle left him, with a very fine red brick house on it, and with Martha's dowry . . . But no, her birthday came and went without so much as a call from him. She will not look at anyone else, so it is whistling into the wind to discuss it." This was by no means an invitation to change the subject, nor did her companion take it for one.

"If my Kate ever brings her young man up to scratch, it will be a wonder, for he has been completely neglecting her lately, too," Mrs. Daugherty admitted.

The ladies exchanged a look of mutual understanding and angry sympathy at the sad plight of their daughters. "Alice is in the same boat," Mrs. Meacham declared, though Alice was only eighteen, and her case was not yet desperate. "Laycombe used to be a very good place to find a husband. Just the right balance between eligible gentlemen and ladies, and with no hesitation at all in coming to the sticking point. We might as well live in a desert for all the chance the girls have now."

Mrs. Daugherty considered the matter a moment in silence and then said, "Do you know, there has not been a *single* marriage in the parish for twelve months, except for Lady Faith Lowrey, and she had to escape to London for the Season to capture her baronet."

"The cause of it all is not hard to find," Mrs. Meacham said grimly. It didn't take a Solomon to know that deterioration had set into the community hard

3

on the heels of Lord Wickham's return to St. Martin's Abbey.

The disappointment had been compounded in that he was extremely eligible himself, since his young wife's demise. Conjecture had been rampant as to which young lady would nab him, but it was now quite clear he was interested in none of the local belles. No, his goal was to turn the thoughts of every bachelor in the neighborhood away from wedded bliss. One could be forgiven for wishing he had put on a turban and stayed amongst the heathens, for he only meant to turn the Abbey into a den of iniquity and Laycombe into a marital desert.

It was grossly unfair, but it was the situation. Lord Wickham had no use for ladies ever since his wife had run off on him with a banker from London. His disgust for marriage, allied to his reputation as the leading buck of the area, had influenced the others. A distinct change had come over the appearance, habits, and pursuits of all the bachelors from the first day Lord Wickham drove his dashing high-perch phaeton, harnessed tandem, into Laycombe; with his face as brown as a blackamoor's, his curled beaver cocked over his eye at a jaunty angle, a natty Belcher kerchief at his neck, and wearing a jacket of a cut never before seen in the village.

Before a week was up, there wasn't a decent white cravat to be seen, not a man of them but had dashed off to London to have his hair cropped *au naturel* and a new jacket made up by Stultz. They none of them quite dared yet to harness three horses to their carriage. Indeed, the ultimate compliment of buying themselves a phaeton and painting it blue had been denied them for financial reasons, but in all other matters they had become Wickham's slaves.

It was Mrs. Meacham's opinion that if Lord Wickham took to wearing bonnets and gowns, the silly nodcocks of Laycombe would dash out to buy up an ell of muslin and a batch of feathers. The pleasant custom of morning calls had been one of the first things to fall by the wayside. Mornings were now taken up in hunting, riding, and other pursuits more suited to wealthy aristocrats than to young men trying to establish themselves in life. Afternoons were given over to horse races, cock-fighting, boxing matches or gathering at the Abbey to view some foreign novelty brought home by Lord Wickham. The social life of Laycombe was all to pieces.

Wickham had spent the three years between his wife's decamping on him and her untimely death, in traveling abroad. According to gossip, for no decent person—certainly no lady—had seen the trophies with her own eyes, he had filled the Abbey with all manner of foreign novelties. There were alleged to be daggers from the Levantine, a strange apparatus for smoking a pipe through a bowl of water, statues and pictures—everyone of them of naked women, and sometimes women and men disporting themselves together without a stitch to their backs. There were samovars (whatever they might be), a whole box of pieces of broken marble from Greece, which someone said, though it must surely be a faradiddle, that Lord Wickham was having pasted back together in his stable.

The way the young gentlemen passed their days was provoking, but their nights were a disgrace and a scandal. Five miles north of Laycombe there was a satanic tavern where, till a year ago, no gentleman would admit he had ever set foot. It was known to hold a gambling hell and purvey blue ruin, and worse, it was a den where fast women lurked. If the local bucks ever *did* enter the place, very likely they might have nipped over once in a while, for boys would be boys and wild oats had to be sown, after all; but if they *did*, they had the decency not to brag about it to anyone but their male friends.

Now Jack Duck's Tavern formed a regular part of their conversation, on those rare occasions when they deigned to call. They thought no more of turning down an invitation to a rout because they had promised Wickham they would go to Jack Duck's Tavern than they thought of combing their hair into their eyes. There was no saying where it would all end, but it was a safe bet it would not end at the altar, and there was the problem.

All this ground had been covered thoroughly by the desperate mothers over the past months, and it was the subject of conversation again that day. "It seems the more their gentlemen disregard and insult the girls, the more eager the goosecaps are to have them," Mrs. Daugherty admitted sadly.

"Worse, the gels think the fault is in themselves," her companion added. "Dallan and Wideman come just often enough to impress Martha and Alice with their new jackets and cropped hair and tales of doings at Jack Duck's place. Martha, like a regular peagoose, quite humbly submitted to Dallan's informing her she was becoming a quiz. I wanted to take the girl and shake some sense into her, but I felt too sorry for her. She had her hair cut and frizzed, burned to pieces actually, by using some new curling iron that Dallan put her onto."

The unfortunate state of Martha's hair received

a sympathetic nod from the vicar's wife. She raised her hand to conceal her words from any passing spies and said, "I am quite sure Kate is using rouge. If her papa ever found out, he would have her locked up in a convent."

"That might be enough to get Andy interested in her again. Clambering up walls and kidnapping a woman would suit the lads down to the heels. Any *decent* attempt to win them is in vain. When Wickham does let the lads off the collar long enough to call, they sit lounging with their legs stretched before them like a pack of Gypsies and ask brazenly for brandy, instead of wine or tea. I am as bad as the girls. I let Martha bully me into buying a bottle of brandy. Wouldn't my Henry turn in his grave to see that! Dallan was so ill-bred as to describe a cockfight in horrid detail." She gave a genteel shudder. "And when I asked him to stay and take his mutton with us, he said he was dining at Jack Duck's, if you please. Lord Wickham had hired some Spanish dancer to come and put on a show."

"Not a lewd one, I hope!" the vicar's wife inquired eagerly.

"A female dancer—no doubt it was a lecherous performance. If he said 'famous good sport' once, he must have said it a dozen times. Dallan is cultivating a set of brown stains on his fingers from taking snuff, and Wideman admitted—or boasted—to Alice that he was now smoking cheroots."

Mrs. Daugherty had ill news to report of Kate's young man as well. "Andy Sproule is contemplating a trip to Turkey, and with this project in mind, he is trying to get his hands on a hogshead of opium and a book on the Muslim religion. You may imagine how the vicar would like that if he ever found out! 'Famous good sport,' he calls this plan as well."

7

"I think the whole lot of them have run mad," her friend declared.

The effects of Lord Wickham's reign were obvious and malign, but of Wickham himself, the ladies saw little. His blue high-perch phaeton was spotted occasionally, darting through the countryside at a reckless pace, frightening children and endangering other drivers. He had been seen in the village on an Arab stallion, usually on Saturday morning. On these rare forays into Laycombe, he scarcely nodded to his erstwhile friends and ignored the young ladies entirely. He attended no balls or assemblies, certainly never darkened the door of the church. He was known to be on calling terms with the Lowreys, connections of his mama, and the same family who had successfully launched Lady Faith. That and ruining all the local sons were the extent of his civility. His coming home, that had promised so much in the way of sociability, had turned out to be an unmitigated disaster, and the question recurred, what was to be done about it?

"All one's relatives' girls being tidily married off at seventeen and eighteen, and one's own daughters left to twiddle their thumbs, and ruin their hair and sigh over as ramshackle a set of young fellows as ever darkened a person's door," Mrs. Meacham scolded. Her eye fell on a letter on the chair-side table and she took it up to relate its contents to Mrs. Daugherty. It was from her late husband's sister, Mrs. Dorman, bragging about the clever match her youngest had made. Cousin Cecilia Cummings, she mentioned, was to be the bridesmaid. Cousin Cecilia had been visiting them for three months and had apparently been instrumental in bringing about the match.

When the letter had been discussed, Mrs. Daugherty finished her tea and left. Mrs. Meacham sat on alone, brooding. Cousin Cecilia—the name rang a familiar bell. Had not Cousin Cecilia also been instrumental in arranging the match for Cousin Kilgour's daughter last year? With nothing better to do, she instituted a search for the old letter. She was of that class of lady who never discarded anything, and the letter was surely still about the house. Her eye roved from marble mantelpiece to mahogany table, but of course the letter would not be in the saloon. She bustled off to the Queen Anne desk in her study and after five minutes' rooting amidst a welter of bills, letters, and receipts, she found it and perused the relevant passage.

"Dear Cousin Cecilia must take credit for the whole affair. She is a wonderful matchmaker. If ever you run into difficulty in getting your girls popped off, you cannot do better than invite Cecilia Cummings for a visit. She knows just how to manage these affairs—a regular little wizard." Her eyes rested on the paper. It seemed almost an omen, that she had remembered the letter and found it, for in the usual way, one could never find anything when she wanted it.

She returned to the saloon and reread the letter from Mrs. Dorman, pausing over the name Cecilia. "They had had a falling out you must know," she read, "but Cousin Cecilia patched the whole thing up in jig time. She is such a dab in that line. She is not the sort to be sponsoring foolish and romantical love matches where there is inequality of position or fortune. She is very nice in all her requirements." Confirmation, if confirmation were needed, of the efficacy of Cousin Cecilia in arranging matches.

How she could use a Cecilia Cummings to patch

9

the dissolving matches together here in Laycombe! But really, she hardly knew the lady. She was no more than a connection. After ten minutes, she had figured out that Cecilia Cummings was her husband's second cousin once removed. Reference to the Dorman letter told her that Miss Cummings would be returning to Hampshire from Kent in a week's time, to prepare for the London Season. She would be passing within a few miles of Laycombe. What was more natural than that she should be invited to stop in en route? The Season was two weeks away.

Mrs. Meacham went to her study and dashed off a letter in care of Mrs. Dorman, earnestly begging Miss Cummings to spare them a few days. She was uncertain whether or not to mention her own girls' desperate plight and decided to do so in a joking manner. It might be just the thing to tip the scales if Miss Cummings were undecided whether or not to stop. The letter was sent off at once, before she changed her mind. Her next job was to speak to Cook about Sunday dinner. "A nice joint of mutton, but not too big," she said gloomily. The days when she was likely to have two strapping young gentlemen at her Sunday table were long gone.

In Kent, Miss Cummings read the letter, smiled and said pertly to Mrs. Dorman, "She has taken the hint. How glad I am I talked you into giving it. I was afraid I should be bored to flinders at home waiting for the Season to open, for I have got everyone there married off you know, and shan't have a thing to do till my cousin Jennie is old enough to need a husband."

"You could always look about for a match for

yourself, Cecilia," Mrs. Dorman suggested archly. "Going on three and twenty . . ."

"I haven't time for that," Miss Cummings said airily. "I am too busy arranging matches for all my friends and relatives."

"It is odd, as you are such a friend to matrimony, that you avoid it yourself."

"Yes, it is strange, but the cobbler's child always goes unshod, you know, and the matchmaker goes unmatched herself. I enjoy marriage only vicariously. I value my freedom more highly. Only think, I could not have come here to you had I been encumbered with a husband, and nor could I stop at Laycombe and make matches for my cousins there. It is fine for some, probably most, but I confess I have never met a gentleman worth giving up my freedom for."

"But have you never been in love?"

Miss Cummings gave the question a moment's consideration. "I have been temporarily infatuated. But it would be a sad mistake to marry while in love—unless the man was unexceptionable as to position and fortune and so on. Lovers are blind, they say, and there seems to be some truth in the matter. And the children can blind their parents, too. That is why I think it wise to have an objective third person involved in making the matches."

"So you say now, Cousin. I doubt you will remain so reasonable when Cupid points his arrow in your direction."

Miss Cummings smiled and paid no heed to the warning. It was old news to her, but she had no fear on that score. She had never loved an eligible parti and had had the wits not to marry any other sort. She was quite content that fate had chosen her to settle matches for others.

11

Chapter Two

MRS. MEACHAM'S HOPES FOR SEEING HER DAUGH-
ters established had sunk low, but not so low that
she intended admitting to a soul that she had
sought outside help. Even her own daughters were
to be kept in the dark, and she must therefore have
a private coze with Miss Cummings as soon as she
arrived. Miss Cummings's letter said she would
come at four. Mrs. Meacham told her girls she
would not be arriving till evening, and she sent
them off to the vicarage to visit Kate and take dinner there.

Miss Cummings was a prompt visitor. At five
minutes before four, she alighted from a very handsome traveling carriage with her abigail, a tall,
fierce-looking dame who answered to the unflattering name of Miss Miser. Miss Cummings came trip-
ping in, embraced her hostess as if they had been
bosom bows forever, and said with no preamble,
"Where are your girls, Cousin? I am dying to meet
them."

Though she was top of the trees herself, Miss
Cummings realized at a glance that her hostess was
a deep-dyed provincial. The saloon, with every ta-
bletop holding a gaudy assortment of bibelots, told

her; Mrs. Meacham's gown and coiffeur and manner told her. None of it mattered in the least. She had no doubt the prospective bridegrooms would be cut from the same bolt, and equality of position was the thing that insured at least a chance of happiness.

Mrs. Meacham led her guest into the Gold Saloon and closed the door to disclose her business in private. As her eyes roamed over her husband's second cousin once removed, she deeply regretted that so little of the family elegance had been transmitted to Henry's daughters. Before her stood a tall, fashionable lady with smooth black hair, wide-set, heavily fringed gray eyes of unusual brilliance, and an enviable complexion. She looked a trifle willful about the mouth, but the voice that issued from the mouth was low pitched and pleasantly musical. Even after the horrors of travel, Miss Cummings appeared completely relaxed, with a blush of pink on her cheeks and a sparkle in her eyes.

She wore a very dashing bonnet and a deep cherry traveling suit that was surely the work of a French seamstress. It clung to high bosoms and a tiny waist. With such an Incomparable as this in their midst, Mrs. Meacham could not think the local beaux would be inclined to offer for their former flirts. She feared she had made a dreadful error, till she recalled the relatives who had received help through the marital machinations of Miss Cummings.

They were seated, a glass of wine offered, and, taking a deep breath, Mrs. Meacham unfolded her tale. "I have purposely sent the girls out visiting that I might have a private chat with you first, Miss Cummings."

"Do call me Cousin Cecilia, ma'am," the dasher

13

invited. She liked to establish a footing of intimacy as soon as possible, as the truth was more likely to be forthcoming then.

"I have formed the decision that the girls must know nothing of the reason for your coming. That is, you are just here to visit, of course, but . . ."

"No, no. I am come to make a match for Martha and Alice," she said quite frankly. "It will be a great pleasure for me. You have not told the girls why I am here then?"

"To be sure, I have not. They are such rattlepates they would tell the whole world, and what a paper-skull I should look."

A furrow creased Miss Cumming's broad white brow. "It will be difficult to get them to cooperate if they do not know why I am here."

"As to that, they will do anything you tell them."

"Biddable, are they?"

"Greenheads, both of them."

"That is a mixed blessing," Miss Cummings remarked, idly drawing off a pair of black kid gloves to reveal shapely white fingers, with a fine diamond ring on her right hand. "If they will be bidden by us, they will also be led by their beaux. I comprehend from your letter you already have two gentlemen in mind?"

"The girls have, and their papa approved before he passed away."

"How are the gentlemen situated as to fortune?"

The affair was outlined in an open manner. Cousin Cecilia accepted her reason for being here so nonchalantly and spoke so calmly of it all that before Mrs. Meacham quite knew what she was about, she had taken Cecilia into her complete confidence. Cecilia nodded, satisfied that the matches were suitable in all external details. Over dinner, every folly was gone into, and it was soon clear to Cecilia that Lord Wickham was the maker of mischief in the case. The beaux had behaved properly in the past, therefore their natures were good. Wickham was leading them astray. She must learn more of this troublemaker.

"I recall the name, though I cannot say I have ever met Wickham," she said pensively. "I believe he married the year before I made my curtsy at St. James's. There was some scandal in the family, was there not?" This, too, was told in colorful detail.

"I have not had a case of just this sort before," Miss Cummings admitted. "When an older gentleman of such high rank is ape-leading youngsters, they will look to him for guidance. My first move must be to meet Lord Wickham and take his measure."

"Well now, that you won't, my dear, for no one visits him, and he never goes anywhere that you might bump into him in the regular way."

Miss Cummings looked surprised. "The young gentlemen met him; he cannot be such a hermit as that."

"Hermit! Ha, if he is a hermit, I am a duchess. What I meant is I cannot introduce you, nor can anyone else. He only visits the Lowreys, and they hold themselves very high. Lord Wickham just rackets around the countryside with all the young bachelors at his heels like hounds after a fox, and how a young lady might make his acquaintance, I am sure *I* don't know. Are we dished before we begin?" she asked, with a helpless look.

Miss Cummings smiled calmly. "Certainly not. The case may be difficult, but it is not impossible. Your daughters know the gentlemen, and the gentlemen know Lord Wickham. If something cannot be contrived to bring us all together, then I shall go riding up to the Abbey myself and ask an interview with him."

Mrs. Meacham's face turned bright pink. "You must never think of such a thing!"

"I have already thought of it, ma'am. Desperate cases require desperate remedies. That is not to say I shall be obvious. My carriage shall lose a wheel, or I shall be so foolish as to go gathering flowers when a storm is about to break, or do any of half a dozen things that will get me into the Abbey fast enough," she explained nonchalantly.

"But would you get out again unharmed?" Mrs. Meacham demanded, with a sage look.

Again Miss Cummings looked surprised. "I thought the problem was that Lord Wickham had no interest in ladies. Do you mean he is a womanizer? That will require a different approach entirely."

"He has no interest in *proper* ladies; as to the other sort, he is a regular Don Juan."

"I see what it is," Miss Cummings said, nodding her head. "He dislikes marriage. His wife's running off on him would account for that. Having made a botch of it himself, he is determined to stamp out the institution. I doubt he would ban horse racing if he took one tumble. What an idiot the man must be."

"I have nothing against *his* not marrying, but why must he go sticking a spoke in Martha's and Alice's wheel?" the irate mother demanded.

"I really must meet him to satisfy myself how to approach the matter," Miss Cummings said. "Now, help me to decide how it is to be done."

"I fear it is impossible."

Miss Cummings realized that the meeting would

have to be a highly irregular one, and said no more of it to her hostess. She inquired after the girls instead, and this formed their conversation till a bustle in the hall announced the daughters' arrival in person.

Cecilia observed them with the sharp eye of a horse trader. She saw at a glance that their charms were provincial charms, as she had anticipated. Martha, the elder, taller, and prettier of the two, was not an ill-formed girl. Her hair was sadly frizzed to be sure, and her gown not well chosen to compliment her pale complexion. A washed-out yellow gown never became anyone, and on a pale blonde it was a catastrophe. The blue eyes were fine, though, and but for an unfortunate tendency to bite her fingernails and speak very little, she would do well enough for a country buck.

Alice was not so well built. She was of short and stocky proportions, with Martha's blond hair shading into red. Worse, a smattering of freckles decked her snub nose. But her smile was sweet, and there was a certain gamine charm about her. Of the two, she had more liveliness, more conversation, more ease of manners. Strange that the prettier girl was less at ease. With the dowries their mother had mentioned, Cecilia thought the gentlemen must be hard cases, indeed, to be so dilatory in their courting.

After answering the requisite inquiries about her trip and the recent wedding, Cecilia began an adroit quizzing about the girls' beaux, to learn how they managed the situation.

The names Henley Dallan and George Wideman were elicited with no difficulty, and from the blushes that accompanied the admissions, the girls' state of infatuation was evident. This infatuation must be diluted a little, to let them see their gentlemen more objectively. Cecilia couched her questions in a manner that implied she took the gentlemen to be older, richer, more handsome, and in every respect more desirable than she knew them to be.

"Only a small estate," she said when Martha mentioned Mr. Dallan's inheritance. "But then he is running so hard after you that you cannot escape him, I daresay," she laughed lightly. "He will do well to get you. He is fortunate, indeed, that you, with fifteen thousand pounds, look no higher for a match. In London, ten thousand usually gets a baronet," she said. "But those terribly handsome men are spoilt from having all the girls chasing them. Lord Byron was the same, in London. Mr. Dallan is a regular corsair, I collect?"

Martha thought perhaps Lord Wickham might be a corsair. A generous viewer might call Mr. Dallan handsome. No one who knew him had ever called him "terribly handsome." She was beginning to wonder what her cousin would think when she met him. "He is not so terribly handsome," she said, with an air of apology.

Cecilia looked at her and blinked. "Ah, it is not his fortune and not his face that have caught you. He is a singularly talented gentleman, I collect? A scholar, who distinguished himself at Oxford? Does he translate the works of Ovid and Virgil into English in clever, polished couplets?" Martha only stared in confusion. "Or is he artistically inclined? Does he collect artworks and make his small estate a cultural oasis in the desert of Sussex?"

"Oh no, indeed! He did not go to university. He is not an intellectual sort of man at all. He rides a great deal, and—and he dances well," she finished weakly.

"But one does not marry a dancing master," Cecilia exclaimed, and looked on in feigned astonishment. Hoping to have given her cousin the notion that she was much too good for Mr. Dallan, she then turned and pulled the same stunt on Alice. It was clear that the ladies had much too high an opinion of their young men and much too low an opinion of themselves. She must buck up their confidence a little.

As a clincher, she asked, "How long do you plan to keep your beaux dangling at your apron strings before you accept them, ladies? You, Martha, must be nearly nineteen," she said cunningly, knowing she was older. "You must be eager to be settled. Why do you not accept Mr. Dallan, as you have decided to have him in spite of . . . that is . . . since you have decided he will suit you?"

"She's twenty!" Alice crowed, and laughed.

"Oh, I am sorry!" Cecilia exclaimed, as though shocked that such antiquity should still be unattached. "Then I collect the match will be rushed forward immediately? A pity your papa's passing away delayed it."

"It is not settled," Miss Meacham admitted, with terrible embarrassment.

"You have not quite decided to have him," Cecilia said. "Truth to tell, I am relieved to hear it, for I am sure you could do better for yourself."

"It's not that, exactly," Martha said, turning redder by the moment.

Miss Cummings felt very sorry for her predicament, but she was ruthless in her tactics. "Oh fie, Mrs. Meacham," she said, turning to the mother. "You are the dragon in the case. You must have

19

pity on the poor fellow. I daresay he is pining his nights away in regret."

Mrs. Meacham was beginning to understand Cecilia's scheme and said, "Lord bless me, I would not forbid the match if he offered."

" 'If' he offered!" Cecilia asked, in a stunned voice. "Good God! Am I to understand . . . Oh I *do* beg your pardon, Cousin Martha. I had no notion. Indeed, I am sorry."

Mrs. Meacham bit back a reluctant smile. This young lady ought to be starring at Drury Lane. She acted as sweet as sugar water, but there was a squirt of lemon in her. Wouldn't she love to see Miss Cummings land Dallan a facer! Into the heavy silence, a little feeling of anger crept. One could almost feel it, and certainly anyone could see it glinting in Martha's blue eyes. Cecilia hoped it would find its rightful target and not settle on herself.

"I did not say I would have him if he *did* offer," Martha said suddenly. Such a view of the matter as her cousin outlined had never entered her humble head before. She felt stupid and cheap to have been pining after Henley Dallan for so long. For four years she had been mooning after him, grateful for any crumb in the way of dalliance. Her spine stiffened, and some semblance of pride could be traced on her face. "In fact, I do not care for him as much as I used to. Since Lord Wickham came to the Abbey, Henley is acting quite stupid. And so is George," she added to her sister, to dissipate the blame.

Here was getting the thing off on the right foot! Cecilia gave every encouragement to their anger and laughed aloud at every folly the gentlemen (whom she decided to call boys) had committed. Alice joined fully in the disparagement, and before the ladies climbed the stairs to bed, there was a fine new flow of spirits in the air. There was no despondency, no sense of helplessness that they would never receive an offer, but rather a question as to whether they would bother to say yes when the offer came.

To be sure and, the feeling dissipated somewhat when the sisters were alone in their beds, without the sparkling eyes of Cousin Cecilia laughing and making them feel very special. But still, a seed had been planted. They were roused to resentment at least at being made to look a fool in front of her. Oddly, neither sister noticed that Cecilia had reached the ripe old age of two and twenty herself without having attached a beau.

Down the hall in the green guest suite, Miss Cummings sat at a desk, writing out in a businesslike manner a list of points to consider. Like a general assembling and planning the maneuvering of her forces, she laid out her plan. At the top of the list stood the name Lord Wickham, with a bold question mark after it. Details of improvement to the ladies' toilettes followed, social functions where maneuvers could be engaged in, and at the end of the list, alone, stood the word "competition." There was half the problem. The beaux required some competition. Whether it was available locally or had to be imported was something to be discovered.

At eleven, she went to bed, satisfied that she had the battle plan under control. *Esprit de corps* at least had improved already since Cousin Cecilia's coming. Lord Wickham was seen as Napoleon to her Wellington at Waterloo. She looked forward to engaging him in battle.

Chapter Three

OVER A HEARTY BREAKFAST OF GAMMON AND EGGS the next morning, the ladies discussed plans for their day. The sisters proposed a tour of the High Street, with a visit to the shops. No female visitor could be expected to delay this delightful excursion. Mrs. Meacham suggested visiting the vicar and other friends to present Miss Cummings to them. All these proposals ended with the words, "This afternoon, of course, for someone might call this morning."

"Surely you do not receive calls every morning? Whom are you expecting to call?" Miss Cummings inquired.

"No one in particular," Martha replied evasively.

"No, no one special," Alice confirmed, "but there is no saying. Someone might drop in."

When the sisters exchanged a furtive glance, Cecilia understood their meaning without being told. "Ladies, you cannot mean you sit home *every* morning on the off-chance that one or the other of your beaux might do you the honor of popping in unannounced for half an hour!" Their sheepish looks told her this was precisely the case, and their insistence told her that one lecture had not sufficed to firm their resolution.

"It is usually in the morning that they come," Alice explained.

"Do they come every morning?"

"Oh no," Martha said. "Usually they go riding or shooting, but if they do call, it is in the morning. About once a week they come, and last week it was on a Tuesday. Since today is Tuesday . . ."

"I hope they come on Tuesday this week, too," Cecilia said firmly, "and you will neither of you be at home to receive them."

"But we can't leave you see, in case they come," Alice said simply.

Cecilia stared in dismay. "My dear goose, you might as well have a sign printed 'DOORMAT' and hang it over your shoulders if this is all the gumption you possess. To sit twiddling your thumbs for weeks on end in case—upon my word, it passes thinking about. Your wits have gone begging, ma'am," she said to Mrs. Meacham, who was looking foolish herself at this point. "How have you let your daughters fall into such a state as this? I was not called a moment too soon if *this* is how you all go on."

"I don't know what ails me," Mrs. Meacham confessed. "I should have given Dallan a sharp word before now. I can give a lady a piece of my mind as easy as buttering toast, but with gentlemen, I feel a heat all over me and don't know which way to look. And besides, it might very likely give Dallan a disgust of us. Henry, my late husband, wanted the match for Martha. They were his dying words. I was all in a pelter, but I kept wits enough to ask him that, and he agreed."

"You will never do as your husband wished with

23

these mealy-mouthed tactics, ma'am. We must fight back."

From that point on, there was no charade about Cecilia being in the house for any purpose but to smarten the girls up and get them both a husband. To this end, she herded them off to her chamber to take them in hand. The first matter was their toilette; an improved appearance was better than a tonic for lifting the spirits. She brought out her fashion magazines and said, "We shall start at the top of your heads. A new hairdo for Martha is first on our list." She said not a word about that dreadful frizz, but it was her intention to remove it.

After looking through the pages, Martha shyly brought her choice to Cecilia. "This one is very dashing," she said.

Cecilia found herself looking at a convoluted mass of swirls and curls and feathers that might be suitable at court, on a sophisticated matron. The fault was her own, for she had used the phrase, "stylish." She worded her refusal softly. "It would take years for your hair to grow long enough for that style, Martha. And in any case, that do is for London dowagers. What do you think of this one?" She indicated a much simpler and more youthful hairdo of soft curls framing the face.

"I like it very much, but my hair won't go like that," was Martha's innocent reply.

"Hair is like men. We shall persuade it," Cecilia laughed, and put the girl into a chair, tied a towel about her shoulders, and began snipping. "I know precisely how this is done, for we had the coiffeur do it to the bride for her wedding, and I asked him to teach me. It is all the crack, I promise you." As she talked, she snipped, till a circle of burnt ends littered the floor.

The next step was to set the curls in papers, and for this chore Miss Miser was called upon. While Martha sat saying "ouch" at frequent intervals, for Miss Miser had a hard hand and pulled till the scalp stung, Alice was taken in hand by Cecilia. Various lotions and unguents were applied to her freckles, finishing with a light coating of rice powder. The freckles did not vanish in one treatment, but they had been softened and did not look unsightly.

While Martha's hair was setting, the sisters were led to their wardrobes to present their gowns for inspection. Some were approved, some were cast aside, and some hung up for alterations, mostly the removal of superfluous gewgaws. The conclusion—music to the girls' ears—was that they needed three new gowns each. In Martha's case especially, the style was to be radically altered. "You are going on twenty-one now, Martha," Cecilia pointed out, "and are old enough to display a little flair, a little sophistication." The fashion magazines were brought forth again, and by dint of repetition and encouragement, Martha was made to realize she could wear something besides pastel colors, laden with ribbons and lace.

"For the next assembly, why do we not have this one made up in a deep royal blue, with that lovely white-fringed shawl you showed me earlier," Cecilia suggested, pointing to the picture of an elegant gown.

Martha examined the picture uncertainly. "But it's so plain on top, with no lace at the neck."

"The better to show off your figure, my dear," Cecilia said frankly. "No one hides her light under a bushel, nor under a clutch of lace and flowers either, if she is clever. These cleaner lines are the highest kick of fashion in London."

Martha worried her lips and frowned. "The color is so dark. I usually wear pink or yellow . . ."

"I'm sure you looked charming in those colors when you were younger, but you are a *woman* now. If you wish Mr. Dallan to take note of the fact, you must look the part, for it seems Mr. Dallan can hardly see what is before his eyes, let alone being hidden from them by countrified fashion."

Mrs. Meacham received a questioning glance from her elder daughter. The mother had put her faith in Cecilia and was in a rollicking good mood at what she had witnessed thus far. "In for a penny, in for a pound. Do as she says."

"And you, Alice," Cecilia continued, "shall wear a white gown with pink ribbons and a few pink rosebuds. I know, you are going to tell me you cannot wear pink with your red hair, but your hair is not red. It is strawberry blond, and pink looks very good on a young girl. And do, for goodness' sake, Martha, take your finger out of your mouth," she said sharply to the elder, for the finger had again found its way into that orifice. Martha withdrew the offending finger and looked apologetic.

The morning passed quickly. The gentlemen did not deign to make an appearance, Tuesday or not. The afternoon was to be spent in selecting material for the new gowns. Martha's curls were not set as tightly as they wished, but the papers were removed anyway, for she would not miss out on the shopping, and she was happy with the result. While adding a much needed air of fashion, they also revealed the pretty contours of her cheeks and jaws.

"My head feels so light," she said, and laughed in pleasure, as she examined herself in the mirror.

Mrs. Meacham accompanied them on the shopping trip. They spent a pleasant hour in Morrisey's

shop, the largest store in the village. It sold drap-
eries and trimmings, gloves and shoes, and was a
haberdashery besides. The ladies spent a long time
mulling over the fabrics and trims, and meeting
friends. Mrs. Meacham got caught up in the excitement and was coerced into buying an ell of ecru
crepe for herself. "I no more need it than I need a
cold in the head," she asserted, but she smiled as
the material was measured out.

It was while they were shopping that a tall, dark
gentleman strolled into the store and stood, waiting
impatiently to be served. With the important matter of competition for the girls' suitors in mind, Cecilia examined him surreptitiously from the corner
of her eye. He must be married, was her immediate
conclusion, or Mrs. Meacham would have mentioned him.

Everything about the man was of the first stare,
from his stylish barbering to his blue jacket of su-
perfine, to his fawn trousers and polished Hessians.
Cecilia moved along to a box of buttons at that end
of the counter that would permit her to see his face.
He was a little older than she had first thought, but
not too old to provide some competition. Fine lines
traced a path across the forehead of a weathered
face. Dark eyes, a strong aquiline nose, a squared
jaw and chin, gave an impression of masculine
strength. It was the infinitely bored expression that
suggested arrogance. One would think to look at
him that he had been waiting a fortnight to be
served, instead of two minutes. Cecilia failed to notice the dotted Belcher at his throat.

"I have come to pick up the York tan gloves I
was fitted for, Mr. Taylor," he called impatiently
over the ladies' heads, in a voice of authority. There
was that in his voice that said, Heed me. I am a

27

man and too busy to wait while these ladies chatter amongst themselves.

That he ordered his gloves custom-made told Cecilia he was not an ordinary customer. She waited to hear if the clerk used the man's name, but he didn't. He just nodded and went to find the gloves. She decided to approach the counter, for she must certainly hear his name when he paid or see it when he signed the account. As she turned, the corner of her reticule caught the tip of the button box and sent it flying across the room. Dozens of bone buttons skittered and bounced across the floor.

"How clumsy of me!" she exclaimed.

The man turned and saw her for the first time. Ignoring the buttons, he examined her face for longer than was quite polite. His penetrating stare took in every feature of her face before flickering quickly down over her gown and even her feet. Cecilia boldly returned stare for stare.

Cecilia was just beginning to feel a stir of anger at his prolonged examination when he smiled and stepped forward. "Allow me," he said, and reached down to retrieve the box. A nice smile, she thought, and nice manners, too, despite that touch of arrogance.

Mr. Taylor came hurrying forward to assure them the shop boy would pick up the buttons. "You are come for your gloves, sir. Sorry to keep you waiting." Mr. Taylor's manner confirmed for Cecilia that the customer was a valued one. She waited with rising interest to hear his name.

"Let the young lady go first," the man said in a well-modulated voice and a perfectly civil tone.

"No, no. You are in a hurry. You go first," Cecilia said.

"I am not in that great a hurry—now." He added

the last word deliberately, while his smile told her he wished to prolong the chance meeting.

"You must not wait on me," she said. "I have been here an age and may be another half hour yet. My friends are buying a great many things."

"I'll just get your gloves," Mr. Taylor said, and darted off.

She was now alone with the stranger, and as the buttons had acted as a sort of introduction, she had no thought of retiring, but rather wished to learn more of him than that he favored a York tan glove. He smiled once again, and when she returned the compliment, he ventured to say, "Are you a tourist in the village, ma'am? You cannot be a resident, for I am a native myself and don't recognize you."

Her hopes soared to hear he lived nearby. His manner, that had a touch of flirtation, suggested he was either a bachelor or an unconscionable flirt.

"I am visiting my cousins, the Meachams," she replied with no hesitation. "Perhaps you are acquainted with them? That is the family over there." She pointed to the fabrics section, where the ladies were still busy, though sparing curious glances at Cecilia.

He turned and looked at the group. "I am a little acquainted with Mrs. Meacham. Are those her daughters?"

"Yes."

"They have grown up since last I saw them. Do you make a long visit?" He showed no interest whatsoever in the daughters.

"I have not determined the length of my visit. Of course, I must be in London for at least part of the Season."

"I hope your visit will not be too brief," he said.

"May I hope we meet again—at the local assembly, perhaps?"

"I cannot prevent your *hoping*," she replied archly.

"You can prevent my hoping in vain."

"I shall certainly attend the assembly." The next step would surely be an exchange of names. Just before it occurred, Mr. Taylor returned.

"Here are your gloves, milord," he said, handing them over. "Perhaps you would like to slip them on."

The man turned away from Cecilia, for which she was grateful. She would not want him to see her goggling like a provincial. Milord! Was he one of the Lowreys Mrs. Meacham had mentioned? The daughter was spoken of as Lady Faith, so her brother—if she had a brother—would be a lord. While her mind roiled with possibilities, the sale of the gloves continued.

"These seem fine," the man said.

"Just flex your fingers, Lord Wickham, and see if the fingers are roomy enough for driving."

Lord Wickham! Cecilia was shocked to the marrow of her bones that this fine buck was none other than the cause of all the marital problems, her Napoleon. She had expected an older, more dissipated gentleman. And after hearing his views on ladies, she had certainly not expected to be favored with any flirtation. Yet her face showed no trace of her astonishment. She even held her ground, to see if she could discover anything more of him.

"I am happy to hear you will be at the assembly. I hope you will save me a dance," Lord Wickham said, as he flexed his hand within the glove.

"I look forward to it," Cecilia smiled.

Then he turned to the clerk. "These are fine. Just

put them on my account." The clerk left; there was really nothing more to keep Lord Wickham in the shop, but still he lingered. "If you have been listening at all, you now know my name. Will you not buy a few buttons so that Mr. Taylor can reveal yours?" he asked. Definitely the man was flirting with her and doing it very well, too, for a gentleman who had the reputation of disliking proper ladies.

"Why it is no secret, milord. I am Miss Cummings."

"Miss Cummings." He bowed formally. "It has been a great pleasure to make your acquaintance. I look forward to renewing it in the near future."

As he had bowed, Cecilia curtsied and smiled, but did not make any verbal reply. Lord Wickham left, and she was immediately joined by the entire Meacham family.

"That was him!" Mrs. Meacham exclaimed, in a voice loud enough to turn heads two aisles away. "He bowed on his way out, and said, 'How do you do, ma'am.' Fancy!" As it was the greatest recognition he had bestowed on her since his return, she was much taken with it. Cecilia thought the lady was easily pleased, if this scanty recognition was to undo the harm of a year's neglect and mischief to her daughters' suitors.

"Pray, lower your voice, Cousin," Cecilia urged.

The whole group thronged to the window, hoping for a glimpse of either black stallion or blue phaeton. Lord Wickham retired on foot, robbing them of the pleasure. "Upon my word, that was very civil of him," Mrs. Meacham continued. "And he smiled, too. He cannot be as bad as everyone says."

"We shall soon know. He plans to attend the next assembly and has asked me to give him a dance."

Such a marvelous piece of news could not be digested in silence. "Cecilia! You never mean it! Did you hear that, girls? He has his eye on your cousin, you may lay your life on it. Here we have been racking our useless brains all night trying to scheme how to meet him—"

Cecilia took her arm and bustled her into an empty aisle, but still she rattled on. "The very first day you are here, not in the village twenty-four hours till you have met him. Did you get his measure?"

"Only his hand," Cecilia laughed. "It looked like a size nine glove, but as to the rest of it, it must wait till the assembly. And now, if you are finished shopping, we must have these materials taken home and call in the dressmaker."

"Lord Wickham never attends the assemblies," Martha said.

"He'll attend this one," Cecilia replied, and laughed an exultant little laugh.

Chapter Four

SUCH A MAGNIFICENT CONQUEST AS CECILIA'S GET-
ting Lord Wickham to speak to her kept her in high
aroma at Meacham's, and a discussion of it helped
pass the time till the spring assembly on Friday
evening. The week passed pleasantly in prepara-
tion for the dance, with gowns to have made up,
new hairdos to perfect, and some little coaching
in deportment. Martha would persist in chewing
her nails to the quick, and Alice had a sad tendency
to swagger like a gentleman when she walked, instead of swaying like a lady. To correct the former,
Martha had her finger soaked in pine spirits, and
to improve the latter, Alice was required to walk
back in forth in the Gold Saloon with *Guthrie's Ge-
ography* balanced on her head. The saloon rever-
berated with the thump of the book hitting the floor.
Its spine was broken and its cover dog-eared after
two days.

The girls' self-confidence was bolstered by an unaccustomed shower of compliments, and in spite of
a certain reluctance to leave the house in the morning, they were obliged to do so by their cousin Cecilia. This last ploy was futile as the week passed
without a single glimpse of their beaux. Kate

Daugherty came and was presented to Cecilia, and she, too, was set in line to bring her fellow under control. She had not the full benefit of Miss Cummings's talents as she lived under a different roof, but she was a fast learner, and without a lesson, her walk improved. She was taught to apply her rouge much more discreetly. Its use was not discouraged as her complexion was on the sallow side. Not a tallow-faced girl, just pale from lack of exercise. She was undertaking a two mile walk a day to overcome her problem, and in the interval, a judicious use of the rouge pot concealed her lack of color.

Friday came faster than seemed possible. Cecilia did not bother to haul the girls from the house in the morning. She had given up on teaching the gentlemen a lesson by that method so that they were all four, including Mrs. Meacham, sitting in the Gold Saloon when the suitors were announced. Cecilia regretted there was not time to hustle the girls upstairs and pretend they weren't at home. On the whole, she was happy to have a look at the beaux before the assembly. She soon discovered that Henley Dallan was the more in need of a lesson than the other.

He was older, better looking, and more full of his own consequence than Wideman. Cecilia thought him a sort of caricature of Lord Wickham—less tall, less dark, much less elegant, but of the same general type. He swaggered in with his shoulders back, a loose curl falling over his forehead, and a Belcher kerchief of exotic hues around his neck. Both gentlemen, Miss Cummings noted with a lifted eyebrow, chose to pay their visit in buckskins and top boots.

No sooner were introductions made than Miss

Cummings began her attack. "You gentlemen are kind to take a minute off from work to drop in. I see by your outfits you were not planning a morning call." She looked at their clothes as if they were a pair of scarecrows.

Wideman, a shorter gentleman with sandy hair and hazel eyes, had the grace to blush and pull at the ends of his kerchief. Dallan did no more than slide a lazy brown eye in her direction and smile condescendingly. "Just so," he remarked, in a voice that held something of a sneer.

The promise of a skirmish evaporated. Wideman, who had been looking intently at Alice ever since his entrance, now spoke up. "You look different, Alice," he decided at last. Alice patted her hair, now arranged in a basket of curls held by a blue satin ribbon, and said nothing. "Better," George added.

"I am trying a new hairdo," she said offhandedly.

"I think you are, too, Miss Meacham," George said, turning to observe the elder sister. Henley had not condescended to remark on the change.

"I have had my hair cut," Martha replied, with a shy smile at Dallan.

"Some *idiot* recommended a metal curling iron to poor Miss Meacham," Cecilia announced, well aware that Dallan was responsible. "They were thought to be a marvel some years ago. Everyone has found them to be a disaster."

Dallan said nothing, but let his gaze wander out the window while he played off his airs. He brought forth an enameled snuffbox and applied a pinch to his nose. A theatrical sneeze followed, and a casual, "Excuse." The insolent set of his head and his way of ignoring the group angered Miss Cummings. She wanted to give him a good setdown before he left,

35

and he was already fidgeting impatiently. From the height of his shirt collars and the cut of his jacket, she knew him for an aspiring dandy and hit him in his weakest spot, his personal vanity. Alice soon gave her a nice lead-in by saying to George that she had a new gown for the assembly.

"What a time we had finding a good dressmaker," Cecilia said. "And I see that you gentlemen also have difficulty in finding a decent tailor." She looked narrowly at Mr. Dallan's jacket as she spoke and gave him a smile of sympathy, though she recognized the work of Stultz at a glance.

"Fact," he agreed lazily. "I have all my jackets made up in London. Old Haggerty has no idea how to cut a jacket properly." He tugged at his sleeves as he spoke.

This loud cry for a compliment was ignored. "For hacking about the countryside, the jacket you are wearing is good enough," she said leniently. "And of course you had not planned to call, or you would have changed. May we look forward to seeing one of your London jackets at the assembly, Mr. Dallan?"

At this pointed insult, Mr. Dallan colored up dangerously and bethought himself of a leveler. "I fancy some people don't recognize city tailoring when they see it," he said, straightening his shoulders to give the best view of the artistry of Mr. Stultz.

"Poor tailoring is not confined to the provinces, Mr. Dallan," she assured him. "There are some London tailors—Stultz for instance—who can turn out a creation quite as ill-fitted as anything to be found in Laycombe."

"Stultz?" Mr. Wideman exclaimed in high dudgeon. "Why he made—"

Dallan silenced him with a stare. "Lord Wickham has his jackets cut by Stultz," he announced, as though that clinched the matter.

"Ah yes, the gentleman who has been out of the country a few years. That would account for it, no doubt. Three years ago Stultz was still doing decent work, although he was never the tailor of gentlemen of the first rank. Nowadays, Weston is all the crack."

"Wickham still uses Stultz," Wideman told her, his freckled face the very picture of innocence. Oh yes, George Wideman would be brought to heel with no difficulty. Cecilia almost found herself losing interest in him.

"Really?" Cecilia asked sweetly. "One hears he has picked up the oddest notions abroad. Does he affect oriental garb as well, or does he confine his strange sartorial humors to the work of Mr. Stultz?"

"Wickham is considered the best-dressed gentleman in these parts," Dallan told her.

"But you will put him to the blush when you appear at the assembly in your London jacket," she replied, still demure. "Weston, I expect?"

"I don't use Weston," he said, becoming irate.

"You prefer Scott," she nodded. "Several provincial gentlemen do. He is cheaper, of course."

"The cost is immaterial to me," he retorted angrily. He longed to tell her that Stultz was the first tailor in the land, but it occurred to him that Wickham had mentioned not liking the shoulders of his latest acquisition and he was going to try someone else. The name escaped him.

"But surely, Mr. Dallan, when you have only a modest estate, you must weigh the cost of everything," Cecilia said innocently. "Or are you a large landowner?"

"Seven hundred acres," he exclaimed, growing angrier by the minute.

Again Cecilia smiled in sympathy. "You are wise to have one or two really good jackets. People in straitened circumstances should buy fewer things, but of good quality. It is a saving in the long run."

Cecilia was aware of receiving silent but speaking glances from her cousins, and felt she had gone far enough for an initial encounter. In fact, she decided to leave them all alone, and let them enjoy a good ripping apart of her manners. It would make them feel closer together.

"Speaking of scrimping and saving," she said brightly, "I mean to polish my diamonds for the assembly myself and save three shillings. Good day, gentlemen. So happy to have made your acquaintance, for I believe Alice mentioned you before, Mr. Wideman."

She had every intention of limiting her slight to Dallan to this inference that Martha had *not* mentioned him, but he then had the ill-timed idea of delivering a parting shot of his own.

"I believe Miss Meacham has mentioned you to us also, Miss Cummings. You *did* say, did you not, Martha, that you had a spinster cousin from Hampshire?"

"Indeed, I did not!" Martha objected instantly.

Miss Cummings's hackles were up, and she stopped at the door. "I cannot say I have ever heard you mentioned, Mr. Dallan, but then there are some acquaintances one does not boast of. Good day." She waited till the door was closed behind her before emitting a gurgle of laughter. The impudence of the puppy! Spinster!

She was no sooner out the door than Dallan gave vent to his spleen. "Pity you have that lady battening herself on you," he said to Martha. "How long does she mean to stay?"

"Not very long, I think," Martha said apologetically. Her finger found its way to her mouth as she thought about Cecilia. She had never mentioned her to Henley. He had called Cecilia a spinster in spite.

"I hope she leaves soon. I for one do not plan to call and be insulted while she remains with you."

"You shouldn't have called her a spinster," Alice said.

"She's a quarter century if she's a day," he asserted, and looked to hear her true age.

"How do you conjure out that, Henley?" Wideman asked innocently, and received no reply. "She's very pretty," he added. He had heard from Lord Wickham that a regular dasher was visiting the Meachams, and so had Henley. It was the main reason they had come, to make her acquaintance.

Recalling all this, Dallan began to tuck in his horns. "She is well enough for an older lady," he conceded.

"She is very fashionable," Martha told him, knowing his love of fashion. "She always visits London for the Season and knows all the smarts and swells."

It was no more than Dallan suspected, and he was particularly ill-humored that he had come to cuffs with the charmer, whom he had hoped to set up a flirtation with. Certainly Wickham had been impressed with her. "I suppose she is well greased. She mentioned wearing diamonds."

"Her papa is a regular nabob," Mrs. Meacham told him. "He owns half of Hampshire. She has two brothers who will get the bulk of the estates, but she has thirty thousand in her own right."

"How old a lady is she?" he asked, eager to hear just how outstanding a prize he had come to cuffs with.

"Twenty-two," the mother said.

Dallan was twenty-five. It formed no part of his plan to marry Miss Cummings. Merely she was to have been a sophisticated diversion. When—if—he ever married, it would be Martha. She was looking jolly today. Sort of distinguished somehow, with that new hairdo and a different gown. There was something else, too, that he could not quite put a finger on. She seemed to be looking at him differently. The unrecognized difference in her mien was calculation, certainly the last thing he would have suspected her of. He did not yet realize that his beloved was measuring him. Even—astonishing thought—finding him lacking in some respects.

That was unkind of Henley to tease Cecilia about being old, Martha thought. He ought not to have called in buckskins and top boots. And having called, he ought to have done more than loll in his chair, take snuff twice without offering his box to George, and look out the window with his back to the company half the time.

"Shall we go on the strut?" Henley asked her.

This was condescension of a high order, and she was not yet strong enough to resist the treat. She went for her bonnet, and the two young couples went out to walk to the village church and amble through the small graveyard, and they never once reflected that this was their own ultimate destination, in some few years.

Martha even entertained, for a half hour, the delightful notion that the gentlemen meant to remain to luncheon, but this was pushing compliability too far. They left the ladies at the door, with assurances of seeing them at the assembly.

The visit was the occasion of a long gossip about the gentlemen, for the girls had to hear Cecilia's opinion of them. She gave moderate approval, but did not let her praise reach any rarefied heights. In fact, she had taken Dallan in such dislike that she decided he must be supplanted, and meant to con alternative possibilities at the assembly. When the girls left, she and Mrs. Meacham continued talking.

"You sent young Dallan to the right about," Mrs. Meacham congratulated.

"And vice versa, ma'am—calling me a spinster!"

"I call that dig downright shabby."

"His manners are really atrocious."

"So they are, but you must pay him no mind. I'm sure you could marry where you liked."

"He won't be an easy man for Martha to live with."

"Not the easiest. I don't know what maggot you have got in your head, Cecilia, wasting your time making matches for everyone else and never a mite of thanks will you get for it either."

"I enjoy doing it. Do you really think Dallan—"

"Henry wanted it."

That was always the last word. Cecilia saw they were not communicating and went upstairs. The afternoon was spent in preparations for the evening party and receiving a call from Kate Daugherty. Mrs. Meacham was her usual chaperon for such outings as the assembly, which the vicar and his wife did not wish to attend.

By dinnertime, the new gowns were in readiness, the coiffures properly set, a glass of sherry drunk to settle their nerves and hopefully brighten their cheeks. After dinner they called the carriage and stopped at the vicarage to pick up Kate. At eight-thirty they all stepped into the parish hall and deposited their pelisses in the waiting room, tidied their hair and gowns, and went on into the dance hall, pulses racing with anticipation of the evening.

Chapter Five

CECILIA NOTICED AT ONCE THAT THE ASSEMBLY HALL was little better than a barn. It was a large, bleak, cold room, lacking even curtains. Black, glinting windows along the length of two walls gave a ghostly reflection of the crowded room. But she was soon distracted by the pleasant murmur and bustle of the crowd. Whether at a private ball in a stately home or at a country assembly, there was always that air of suppressed excitement, of waiting, and wondering what the evening would bring.

The ladies' toilettes must be examined and compared, and the gentlemen observed in hopes of an interesting newcomer. On the ladies there were many adornments: a surfeit of floss trimming, tinseled silk turbans and strass glass jewelry. Cecilia found herself scanning the crowd for a tall, dark gentleman who wore a size nine glove. She was sure he would stand out in this countrified throng, but she did not see him.

The object of most outstanding interest was, in fact, herself. Mrs. Meacham's visitor had been glimpsed in shops and introduced to a select few, but this was her first public appearance. She had not been seen before decked out in diamonds and a gown designed in Paris, and a gown of such magnificence that all the ladies gaped in envious pleasure. Beneath a rose-lace overdress, a glimmer of cream satin was to be seen. Her raven curls bounced in saucy abandon, with only a small diamond star over the left ear to restrain them. This casual use of diamonds was a new thing entirely in Laycombe. Miss Cummings and her grand toilette would provide gossip for a week.

Gossip was soon enriched by an item of even greater interest when Lord Wickham strolled in. The village had had little more than a glimpse of him either, and now they would have five hours in which to take in any foreign tricks he had picked up during his travels. His haircut, done in London, was thought to have something of old Rome in it. He had traded in his *au naturel* for a Brutus cut. His complexion, darkened by Albion's wind and rain, suggested to local eyes the sun of Egypt. The ruby nestled in the folds of an intricate cravat was credited to Turkey. When he walked directly to Mrs. Meacham and bowed punctiliously over her hand, there was thought to be something Gallic in his posture. And when he led Miss Cummings into the first dance, many a wise head nodded and inferred silently, "I thought as much."

Miss Cummings had rather thought the same herself and had polished her diamonds and worn her best gown for no other reason than to impress Lord Wickham. The tricks she purveyed to her charges were the same ones practiced by herself. She had decided she would set up a flirtation with him to get into his confidence and direct his interests in the proper course, to help along her cousins.

She was no stranger to masculine admiration and realized from their first meeting that Lord Wickham was interested in her. When his first object upon entering the hall was to look all around till he spotted her, and his second to come and be presented, she felt the battle half won. The remaining half would be taken care of while they danced. She set out to charm him.

"You see I have kept my word and come to the assembly," she said, with a flirtatious smile.

"I am happy to have the opportunity to continue our chance meeting," he replied, in the same manner. "And how happy the locals are to have someone new to stare at."

Cecilia silently acknowledged that he had noticed she was garnering more than her share of attention, but of course made little of it. "Are you sure it is not yourself that is being quizzed? You are a rara avis here as well. I have heard unflattering tales of your being too toplofty to attend the local dos, sir."

"I'm here, ain't I?" he riposted. "I think you know what has drawn me out of hibernation. Tonight I was promised *you* would be here."

"I don't recall that it was a solemn promise."

"Oh no, not solemn."

The flirtation was off to a fine start. Such attentions as this were mere commonplaces to Miss Cummings. She smiled, believed perhaps a tenth of what he was saying, and forged on. "You would have me believe you are here on the strength of a one minute conversation with a stranger?" she asked archly.

"Mrs. Meacham is a neighbor, and perforce her cousin is not a total stranger. As to that one minute conversation—what a fast pair we are, to have set up an assignation in sixty seconds flat."

"You make it sound as though I had accosted a

45

strange gentleman for no reason but to tell him I would be attending the assembly," she charged. "You asked me if I would be here."

"How else should I have discovered what I wanted to know?" he asked reasonably. "As to that description, 'strange gentleman'! I am not *that* strange. *You* are the one who hurled the buttons all over the shop when you could not get the clerk's attention. I did no more than holler like an auctioneer."

"I knocked the box over by accident. How horrid you are—you make me sound like a monster," she said, and used it as an excuse to pout.

Lord Wickham recognized her every stunt and approved them all. This was no innocent miss, but a high-flyer very much to his taste. "Horrid," he agreed amiably. "And now I mean to be fast as well and ask you an impertinent question. How long do you stay in Laycombe, and when I may call on you?"

"That is two impertinent questions, sir, one of which you have asked before. You were obviously paying no attention whatsoever to my reply. My stay is of an indefinite duration."

"But it is really the other question I am more interested in. When may I call on you? You see my trick, I do not ask *if* I may call, or you might say no."

"A loaded question, in fact. Such ruses are not necessary with me. You may call whenever you wish."

"Carte blanche?" he asked, lifting a black wing of brow. "That is *much* better than I dared to hope."

"I can't say I care for your choice of words, sir. Carte blanche has ambiguous overtones."

"Only when given to ladies by gentlemen, surely?" he quizzed.

"You mean to women, I think. The practice is not in vogue with *ladies*, to my knowledge." The correction was delivered in a bantering way, to remove the sting.

"I stand corrected, ma'am," he said humbly, and immediately ran on to make sport of her. "I have so little knowledge of how affairs of that sort are carried on that I must accede to your superior knowledge."

"Take care, sir, or I shall rescind that generous invitation to call when you wish." Oh dear, was she to begin sitting at home every day, too, waiting for her beau? "Of course," she said hurriedly, "I cannot promise I shall be at home every day."

He lowered his brow and gave a mock frown. "You trifle with me, Miss Cummings. Pretty talking, indeed! Much good my permission to call will do me if I am only to be told at the door that you are out. I do not live in Laycombe, you know, that I may run to your door ten times a day. I live five miles beyond the village. You were not interested enough to inquire, so I volunteer the information gratuitously."

"Shall we leave it to chance?" she suggested. "If you happen to call when I happen to be at home, we shall have a delightful chat." She thought he would press on to make a firm engagement, but he did not. She wouldn't lower herself to pursue the matter, but her pride was piqued.

They made light conversation in those intervals when the steps of the dance permitted, and at the set's conclusion, Lord Wickham offered her a glass of punch, which they took in chairs at the edge of the room, to allow of more involved conversation.

It was then determined officially what Miss Cummings already knew very well: that Lord Wickham has been abroad for three years, was a widower (no details were added to this interesting fact), and that he resided at St. Martin's Abbey. Miss Cummings told Wickham what he had already been at some little pains to discover: namely, that she lived at Ferncote in Hampshire and was single with two brothers. Within three minutes they had taken each other's measure fairly accurately. Two well-to-do, worldly people with no intention of making any serious attachment, but ready for a pleasant flirtation. This done, Cecilia risked a judicious mention of Mr. Dallan and Mr. Wideman.

"Your name arose in conversation this morning," she began. "Mr. Dallan and his friend called on my cousins. You were mentioned as an expert in tailoring," she offered.

"That is not my area of expertise," he said, with a meaningful smile that left no doubt as to his specialty—women.

With his penetrating dark eyes smiling at her, Cecilia felt a warmth invade her bones. Lord Wickham's behavior was bordering on the unacceptable, and she wished to let him know it, without completely quelling his interest. "So I told them," she said vaguely.

"You show an extraordinary lack of interest in me, ma'am," he continued playfully. "Name, address, interests . . ." She gave him a cool look, and he continued blandly, "Dallan could not have chosen a worse field of expertise. I used to frequent Stultz when I was a young buck, and made the error of visiting him to refurbish my wardrobe when I returned from abroad. I find I have outgrown his padded shoulders and nipped waists, and have transferred my custom to Weston. And you, I think," he said, conning her gown with a practiced eye, "have a French modiste. Charming."

"Yes, Mademoiselle Dupuis is all the rage."

"You do her infinite credit."

This was all very fine and flattering, but Mr. Dallan was the subject to be discussed, and she tried again. "Those young gentlemen I mentioned have a very high opinion of you."

"The countryside is thin of company. My old friends have all married or moved on, so I have been racketing around a little with those young fellows. A man cannot stay home with a book every night."

She adopted a sympathetic pose, but stated her point all the same. "It is a pity you have not a more suitable set of friends, for young gentlemen of moderate means could ill afford to keep the pace you set, I think."

"Oh I am not such an expensive fellow as all that," he laughed. "A little racing, a little sport. We find an hour now and then to attend to business. I am not about to ruin them, if that is what you fear."

"It can hardly amount to fear, as I am so little involved, but the ineligibility of yourself being used as their pattern card does cause a question."

He leveled a playful but pointed look at her. "Have you a more suitable companion in mind for me, ma'am?"

Cecilia swallowed a little gush of pleasure at this hint of wishing to spend more time with her. "I hardly know all the local inhabitants yet," her mouth said, but her eyes, which she managed with the skill of a courtesan, gave the answer he desired.

"It is not a local inhabitant I have in mind, but

a visitor," he answered, with the masculine version of the same look.

"Why Lord Wickham, I do believe you are flirting with me!" she charged.

"Is that what they call it nowadays?" he parried. "It used to be called trifling when I went abroad."

Trifling! Well, he could have hardly have told her more plainly that he meant nothing by his gallantry! And he was looking pretty sharp, too, to make sure she caught the full import. "Now it is called an *à suivi* flirtation," she explained. "You are behindhand in the diction regulating society. For shame, and you home for a whole year."

"So long as it is only the diction that has changed, and not the rules, I cannot run too far amok."

"I shouldn't think the rules have changed," she allowed.

Secure that they now understood each other, Lord Wickham continued his attack. "Do you ride at all, Miss Cummings?"

"I enjoy it, but have not brought my mount with me."

"I have several hacks at the Abbey—one quite a gentle goer, if you would like to have the use of her."

"Really you are too kind. I cannot like to accept such a favor from a mere acquaintance, however."

"That presents no insurmountable problem. We have only to shift ourselves forward to the status of friends."

"Yes," she smiled and wafted an elegant feathered fan. "And when we are friends, then I shall be happy to accept the loan of a mount."

"Friendship will best be achieved by meeting

50

again. As your visit is of so indeterminate a duration, I shall bucket ahead at top speed. Shall we say—tomorrow?"

Cecilia gave her assent and concealed like a spy that she had got exactly what she wanted from the evening—to establish a firm footing with Lord Wickham.

The music was striking up again, and she must leave him. Mr. Wideman came forward to claim a dance, and it was with a feeling of satisfaction that Lord Wickham was seen to ask Martha to stand up with him. All the romances were progressing satisfactorily. Martha had had the first dance with Dallan, Alice with Wideman, and Kate Daugherty with Andy Sproule. The evening continued as smoothly as silk, with the same group changing partners amongst themselves. In the corner, Mrs. Meacham congratulated herself on her ingenious idea of asking Cousin Cecilia to visit them. What a marplot she had been not to have taken steps sooner. At this rate, there would be wedding bells before summer.

Some little while later a waltz was announced, and Cecilia again had the pleasure of being sought by Lord Wickham. He had been abroad when the waltz gained popularity, but his natural grace allowed him to perform well, while still continuing the flirtation. "Had I realized England had unfrozen to the extent of allowing a gentleman to hold a lady in his arms in public, I would have returned sooner," he smiled.

"Yet you have waited this long to indulge the pleasure. This is your first assembly."

"Till now there has been no lady I was eager to get into my arms."

The girls had another dance with their beaux, too, and while it was very satisfying, the thought did intrude that they could none of them stand up three times with the same gentleman, so that the excitement was over till supper time. No actual supper invitations had been issued by the gentlemen, but it was taken for granted that the couples would dine together. As the time for supper drew near, the ladies began to look around the hall to give an inviting smile. It was then that Alice exploded her shell.

"We had best get busy and find a partner for dinner," she said.

"I have not seen Henley around for half an hour," Martha said. "I wonder if he stepped out with Andy to blow a cloud."

"No, he has left," Alice said. Everyone stared.

"Left!" Cecilia exclaimed.

"Yes, Lord Wickham has taken them all over to Jack Duck's Tavern. It is the Spanish dancer's last night. That is why they all came so early to the assembly, for lately they have been dropping in around supper time, if they come at all. George told me they meant to get away by eleven."

"What, left without even saying good-bye?" Martha demanded.

"George said to say good night to everyone for him," Alice said.

Cecilia felt a hot surge of anger swell up in her. "Why did you not tell me sooner, that I might have stopped them?" she demanded.

"You couldn't have stopped them, Cousin," Alice told her. "They decided three days ago. The Spanish dancer is very good, and it is her last night. From here she goes on to London. I wish I could see her."

"It is all of a piece," Mrs. Meacham scolded. "I knew it was too good to last."

Martha stuck her finger in her mouth and sulked. "We might as well go home."

"Use your sense, girl!" Cecilia snapped, and removed the offending finger. "They are not the only gentlemen in Laycombe. We must find other partners. Get busy and see what you can do."

They each found a partner, but of such indifferent qualifications that little interest was taken in the dinner hour, and they left before the dance was over. As they drove home in the carriage, Cecilia asked, "Do they often pull this stunt on you?"

"No, they usually come late," Alice reminded her.

"I wish you had told me sooner. When is the next assembly?"

"In two weeks' time," Mrs. Meacham said. "There is one every two weeks in the spring. The rest of the year, it is one a month, with a Christmas party besides."

"It must be the next one then," Cecilia said with determination. Everyone was too weary to inquire her meaning, but they placed faith in her delivering their beaux for the entire evening the next time.

Miss Cummings was not so docile as that. Wickham's trick was seen as an outright attack on her position. Wellington, she felt, would not take it without retaliating. An examination of the local bucks had shown her that competition must be imported. Inferior as Dallan and Wideman were, they were the best of the local lot. But till she had the matter under her control, she would not tell her cousins her plan.

Cocoa was served when they reached home, and over this refreshment the ladies discussed the toilettes, partners and flirtations of all their friends at the ball. When this necessary ritual was over, they went to bed, too fagged to worry about not sleeping.

Chapter Six

IT WAS THE CUSTOM IN LAYCOMBE, AS ELSEWHERE, to sleep in late the morning following an assembly, but with plans to formulate, Cecilia did not sleep in very late. She spent the hour before her cousins' rising in deep thought. At the next assembly, she would repay the gentlemen, not omitting Lord Wickham, for their cavalier treatment. She admitted to no more than a fit of pique at his sheering off. He was no suitor. In fact, the others seemed to consider it an act of great condescension that he had come to the assembly at all.

Lord Wickham aside, how should she retaliate against the others? She could bar—and it would have to be by main force—the girls from attending the next assembly. This no sooner occurred than to be rejected. The occasions when the couples were together were already too few. Besides, it might be recognized as retaliation and she was more subtle than that. What would please her much better would be to have the girls' cards so full that they could barely squeeze Dallan and Wideman in for one dance. And that meant bringing in reinforcements.

London was the obvious place to recruit them.

With the Season drawing nigh, crowds would be gathering, and some of them would agree to spend a few days before the Season at a country party. She jotted down half a dozen names, and felt that if half of them accepted, it would provide a beau each for her cousins and Kate Daugherty.

She debated a moment whether to send the invitations by mail or deliver them in person, and soon opted for the latter. A day in London would provide a pleasant diversion for her cousins. What day should they go? Lord Wickham was to call today, and tomorrow was Sunday. The London crowd would be thin on a Monday, as weekend parties sometimes lasted an extra day. She tentatively settled on Wednesday as the day for the trip. It only remained to get Mrs. Meacham's approval and drop a line to Papa's housekeeper in Hanover Square to prepare the house.

She did not broach her plan the instant her cousins came down to breakfast. There was still some discussion of the assembly to be indulged in. Cecilia received many questions as she had been singled out by Lord Wickham. "What is he like?" was the most often asked one. She patiently repeated that he was very civil, not so very toplofty, and so on.

"I thought him an excellent dancer," Martha said, to remind them that she had been singled out for his second partner. "Better than Henley. Henley was going to ask you to stand up, Cecilia, but he was afraid you would refuse."

"I hope I am not so rude as that! I should have been happy to stand up with him," Cecilia assured her.

"He's taken the notion you dislike him."

Cecilia knew that a feud in that quarter would

only keep Henley away and was quick to mend the quarrel. "Only because I teased him a little about his jacket?" she laughed lightly. "You must tell him I was only funning. I only tease those men I like," she added. "He looked very well, did he not? Quite an unexceptionable jacket he wore last night."

Martha smiled and said she would tell him next time she saw him.

"When will you see him again?" Cecilia asked at once, and heard that no firm call was planned.

"Is there no private party planned for a Saturday night?" she asked, and was told there was none. "A pity local company is so thin. Our wits are gone begging! Why do we not have a party, Mrs. Meacham?" Their shocked faces told her this was innovation of a strong order, to be having a party for no obvious reason.

"They always go to Jack Duck's on Saturday night," Alice announced baldly. "George says it is the best night."

"Then Saturday is precisely the evening we must have our party," Cecilia countered.

"It is too late for this week," Mrs. Meacham mentioned. "We could get it together for next Saturday."

"Excellent. Let us send out the cards this very day. I shall send one to Lord Wickham as well, with your permission, ma'am."

Her hostess looked shocked at the idea. "Oh my dear, we cannot ask *him*!"

"Is he as ramshackle as all that?"

"Nothing of the sort. The hitch is that he never accepts an invitation anywhere. He received many offers when he first returned, but he never accepted them."

Cecilia had no wish to receive a refusal. "You told me he never attended the assemblies either, but he went last night."

"So he did, and it was the greatest surprise in the world. Whoever would have believed it? Everyone spoke of it. And of you, too, Cecilia. You were a great success. But as to his accepting an invitation, that is a cat of a different color. He calls on no one."

"He is calling on me today," Cecilia announced, and received all the astonishment she could wish.

"What, calling here?" the mother asked, and dropped her toast in shock. "You never mean it! Here, at my house."

"I hope you do not mind."

"Mind? It is famous." She slapped her knee in glee. "He never goes anwhere but to Lowreys. How everyone will stare when I tell them. And here I sit like a moonling, when the whole room will have to be turned out." She rose from her chair before anyone could stop her and sent a bevy of servants with beeswax and dust cloths, tea leaves and broom, to clean the immaculate Gold Saloon.

"You have attached him, Cousin," Martha marveled, and in her excitement her finger found its accustomed way to her mouth.

"Which I never would have done had I chewed my fingernails to the quick." Martha removed the finger and smiled an apology. "As to having attached him," Cecilia continued, "it is no such a thing. Merely I am letting him call so that I may exercise a little influence on him, to detach him from your beaux."

"He must be sweet on you," Alice insisted. "He never asked to call on any other girl. Sally Gardner was used to chase him dreadfully—well, she still

58

does. Every time he rides into the village, she flings on her bonnet and pelisse and goes scrambling into the street after him, letting on she needs something in whatever shop he goes into, and accidentally dropping her bags at his feet, so he has to help her pick them up."

"Oh dear," Cecilia laughed. "I hope he doesn't think I was using her stunt Tuesday when the buttons fell."

"You only did it once," Alice said forgivingly. "Sally does it all the time. You remember, Martha, when Lord Wickham's housekeeper broke out into hives and he was several times at the chemist's shop trying to find a remedy, Sally used to scoot into the chemists the minute she spotted him coming down the street. She used to get a teaspoon of clove oil at a time, and her mama didn't have a toothache either because she would be out gallivanting herself the minute Lord Wickham was down the road."

Cecilia smiled ruefully at such gauche behavior, and as soon as Mrs. Meacham returned, she broached the London plan. It met with unanimous approval. When Cecilia asked if she could put a few guests up if they wished to come to the assembly, that, too, was agreed to. The house was the finest in the village, much larger than they needed, with ten bedrooms and two suites. Martha and Alice were thrown into a tizzy to hear that the guests were gentlemen and demanded an accounting of each. As Cecilia had no idea which of her friends would accept, however, she could not oblige them, and made it a mystery.

Cecilia assumed her young cousins would be at home when Lord Wickham called and hoped to put Martha forward a little. She was thwarted in her scheme. Martha and Alice left for the vicarage right after breakfast, to discuss the assembly with Kate, but their mother would be at home.

"He'll come around eleven-thirty," Mrs. Meacham said. "He usually rides into the village at eleven on Saturday morning to tend to any business or shopping or banking he may have before the weekend. After he is finished, he'll stop here."

"You set me down a peg, ma'am," Cecilia said. "I had thought he was making a special trip in to see me."

"So he would have done, had it been any day but Saturday, and he coming anyway. It must be nearly eleven. There goes Sally Gardner with her basket. She times her leaving the house to meet him. Yes, there he is. Why, he is in his phaeton; he usually rides his black horse. A fierce looking animal it is. The lads say it's an Arabian."

"He does not mean to pay his call in riding clothes at least." Her pride was assuaged to see that he had made this concession to her call.

"So I see," Mrs. Meacham said, peering through the sheer curtains. "He is likely getting some things that he will need the carriage to haul home."

"You are determined to deflate my pretentions," Cecilia said, yet her cousin's explanation struck her as plausible. She had been taking too much credit for this call. It was actually no inconvenience to Lord Wickham at all, and therefore little compliment to herself.

The only minor consolation she could derive was that he called before he attended to business. This might indicate an eagerness that the rest of his call did not uphold. When he was seated in the well-dusted Gold Saloon, he addressed the first half of his remarks to Mrs. Meacham.

"You have removed from the Maples since I left," he began, and tendered his sympathy at the cause. "You must have hated to leave it, but you have no sons, as I recall. A large estate is a big handful for a lady."

Mrs. Meacham soon found herself overcoming any shyness and chatting sociably. While they chatted, Cecilia had time to examine his toilette. Wickham was turned out remarkably well for a country gentleman. His shirt front and cravat were immaculate; his Hessians were newly polished, and his jacket was unexceptionable. It was the work of Stultz to be sure, but not one of his more outré creations.

The conversation proceeded with congratulations from Lord Wickham on the beauty of the Meacham girls, and a playful mention that they had got their looks from their mother. This was palpable nonsense; they both favored their father in appearance, but it went down very well. Oh yes, Wickham was definitely setting out to please the dame and having wonderful success, too. Next he complimented her on the house.

"I had the happy idea of having a bow window thrown out, for it gives such a good view of the street. I can see it from end to end. It is something to do of a dull afternoon, looking out on the street."

"A charming idea, and the room is so tastefully decorated, too. My own place has sadly deteriorated, since I have been away. I am trying to bring it back, but that certain touch is lacking. The woman's touch. I hesitate to entertain till I have refurbished the place." The weak pretext was to account for his lack of sociability.

Had this been Lord Wickham's second visit instead of his first, she would certainly have recommended his taking a wife, but she was not yet at that stage of intimacy, and the conversation veered to other topics.

"A charming assembly last night, was it not?" Wickham said, to draw Cecilia into the talk.

"I wonder that you left the party so early, if you liked it," she replied saucily. Her sparkling eyes told him, "You may have cozened her, but I am not so easily fooled."

"Having had my two dances with the most charming lady there, the rest was all futility. Mrs. Meacham will forgive my saying so, I trust. Her own lovely girls are much too young for an old Benedict like myself to presume to show an interest."

Mrs. Meacham would have forgiven him for attempted murder when he was behaving so handsomely. "My two hussies have a certain set of lads in their eye, you must know," she said.

Before Cecilia could turn this opening to any use, a servant appeared with wine and macaroons. Lord Wickham felt he had done the pretty with the hostess and turned his attention fully to the younger lady. "Miss Cummings, you are missing some fine riding weather. A pity you hadn't brought your mount with you."

"Alice has an old cob in the stable. You are welcome to it I'm sure," the hostess mentioned. "Of course Bricks is ancient. The girls don't ride much, since we removed from the Maples."

"I have several mounts at the Abbey, if you would like to borrow one while you are here," he offered.

There was a little chicanery in presenting this as a new idea, for she had already refused the offer the evening before. Cecilia began to understand that his courting of Mrs. Meacham was to make himself appear respectable. The challenging gleam in his eye confirmed her suspicion.

"You are very kind, but I cannot think—"

Mrs. Meacham cut her off in mid-speech. "That is mighty handsome of you, milord. Now there you are, Cecilia. There is plenty of room in the stable, and I can easily spare a groom, so you need not let that hold you back."

"You forget, ma'am, my team are in the stable," Cecilia pointed out.

Mrs. Meacham immediately gave a lengthy enumeration of the stalls, and the cattle in them, and ended up saying, "And that leaves two boxes standing empty all the live long day."

"I'll have Lady sent over this afternoon," Wickham said. A smile of triumph rested on his arrogant face. "A tidy bay mare. Not up to my own weight. I shall accompany you on your first outing, to let you in on her little tricks."

"A tricky one, is she?" Cecilia said, quizzing him boldly. "I wonder why that does not surprise me."

"Well, she *is* a lady," he riposted. Mrs. Meacham frowned at this non sequitur, but no one noticed. "Shall we say tomorrow morning, Miss Cummings?"

"You forget tomorrow is Sunday. We shall be at service in the morning."

"Ah yes, so we shall." A muscular spasm around his mouth betrayed his mood, without quite forming a smile. "Three o'clock then, if that suits you?"

She was torn between a very real desire to ride, and a wish to show Wickham a lesson. He was accustomed to having his own way—that much was patently obvious. He had come in and charmed Mrs. Meacham to do his bidding with a shower of insincere compliments. She wavered a moment, and while she wavered, Mrs. Meacham rushed in and settled the affair.

"There is no need to send Lady over this afternoon, Lord Wickham. Why do you not just bring her with you tomorrow afternoon, and save a trip?"

He shot a triumphant look at Cecilia. "An excellent idea." Before any further demur was possible, he was on his feet, excusing his hasty departure, but he had a meeting with his man of business. A charming visit ... He would call tomorrow at three ... And he was gone.

"Well now, that was mighty handsomely done of him," Mrs. Meacham declared, and glanced at the window. "There goes Sally Gardner again. She is like a dog after a cat. She'll be galled that he was here. Aye, he's fooled her this time. She has no excuse to go barging into his solicitor's office. She'll stay gawking in at the milliner's window next door till he comes out."

Cecilia glanced out the window and saw a sharp-nosed lady of provincial cut, staring at the solicitor's closed door. She wore a frustrated face. "I ought not to have borrowed a mount on such short acquaintance," Cecilia said. She feared she was talking to herself, for her companion had run to the window, monitoring Sally Gardner as closely as Sally was monitoring Wickham.

Mrs. Meacham heard, and answered. "Short acquaintance? You forget I have known Lord Wickham forever. Not well, you know, but as a neighbor. There is nothing in his loaning her to you when he cannot ride her himself. It is a pity he goes so little into society nowadays. Many a fine party was thrown at the Abbey when his wife was alive. She was quite a proverb for hospitality. She had the place done up after her marriage. That was only six years ago. I cannot think it is so bad as he says."

Cecilia took up her embroidery and the two ladies settled into the companion chairs in the embrasure of the bay window for easier surveillance of the High Street. "What was she like?" Cecilia asked.

"Very pretty. Adrianna Heathmore is who she was before marriage. Her papa was a merchant. They say he made a monstrous deal of money in trade, but when they came here, he had sold out and set up as a gentleman on a nice estate about five miles north of the Maples. No one took much note of them at first, but then they sent Adrianna to London to make a debut, and that is where she landed Wickham. Her folks were thrilled to mince meat. She was a blonde girl, very pretty."

Cecilia listened closely. If he liked blondes, then perhaps Martha might interest him. "Did you know her well after her marriage?"

"Not well. She did not mix a great deal with the local crowd. She was back in London on the slightest pretext and had the Abbey full of her and Lord Wickham's friends. We were invited to a few large dos. They seemed a happy couple."

"Why do you suppose she left him? I would not think a merchant's daughter would have any regrets at marrying a lord, and a lord with an Abbey besides. She seemed happy, you say." The idea occurred to her that the heavy partying might have been Wickham's idea. From there it was an easy leap to imagine that he had taken a lover, and that was the cause of the rupture.

Mrs. Meacham had nothing to offer but conjecture. "Everyone thought she must be twopence short of a shilling to do anything so foolish. I expect she found us a dull lot. The man she ran off with— Gregory was his family name—was only a commoner, though a vastly rich man. She ran away with him to Italy—well, she knew her swell London friends would cut her dead. We all thought, when Wickham left, that he had run after her, but it turned out it was not Italy he went to first at all. It was Egypt and Turkey and such outlandish places. She and her Mr. Gregory bought up a villa in Florence, and that is where she died. Of a fever, folks said, but it wouldn't surprise me if she just died of partying every night."

"He does not speak of her at all. I have never even heard him mention her name, though he did say he was a widower. Of course I don't know him well."

"Pride, that is what is keeping him close on the subject. I would not advise you to mention her to him. The Wickhams are all as proud as Spanish grandees. There never was such a scandal in the family before. At least her dying saved the disgrace of a divorce. She never married Gregory, you know, but just lived in sin with him. I don't know how a Christian girl could do it."

A motion in the street distracted her from her story. "He must be coming out. There is Sally dropping a bag of buns all over the street. Ha, she has outdone herself this time. She has dropped a bottle of something, too—it is running down the gutter. What can it be? It looks like marbles. Olives! It is olives, nasty things, all pickled in brine. And here comes Lord Wickham. But she is out of luck. Mr. Cosby is helping her pick up the buns. They'll be brushed off and put on the table, or I miss my bet."

"That one won't see her table," Cecilia said, when a mongrel grabbed one in its jaws and ran off. Lord Wickham entered the cobbler's shop and came out with a long box.

"He is buying a new pair of top boots," Mrs. Meacham conjectured. Cecilia was more interested to notice that he had good reason to drive his phaeton. It wasn't deference to his call on her that caused it.

Their conversation was broken off by the entrance of the girls, back from the vicarage, and eager to hear all about Wickham's visit. They had news of their own to relate as well. Andy Sproule had been at the vicarage. He had seen the Spanish dancer again and was looking forward to the new performer slated for that evening. The gentlemen, including Lord Wickham, planned to return to Jack Duck's again that night. Any good Wickham's visit had done was undone by this disclosure.

"We shall send out the invitations for our rout next Saturday evening," Cecilia said, to keep their spirits up. Her own mood was one of grim determination.

It seemed no less than treachery that Wickham had come to see her, buttering up Mrs. Meacham and slyly arranging to return the next day. Why had he done it? The answer was clear to a six-year-old. He wanted to enjoy a 'trifling' friendship with her, and that would require her hostess's cooperation. He was deceiving Mrs. Meacham into thinking his intentions were honorable, but between themselves, she was to understand it was not to be taken seriously.

Such conniving was hardly a new thing in the world. But it annoyed Cecilia that her best efforts, and she had put forth at least a very good effort, had produced so little effect. Wickham should be a little smitten with her by now. He was a cold, heartless man. She would not make any effort to hand him to Martha. That poor innocent lamb would be torn to shreds by him. He had very likely driven his wife to fleeing. He must be stopped, before he ruined Dallan and Wideman and Sproule. This case was proving to be her most difficult yet. It was because she had three young couples to manage, she told herself. But she knew it was not so. The spoke in her wheel was always Lord Wickham.

Chapter Seven

ONCE LORD WICKHAM'S VISIT WAS OVER, SATURDAY was but an indifferent day, and the evening was dismal. The knowledge that the gentlemen were enjoying themselves at Jack Duck's did nothing to dissipate the gloom. Cecilia spoke bracingly of next Saturday, but no one save herself felt any certainty that next Saturday would be any better than this one. There was a feeling afoot, not actually stated but inferred, that Cecilia was making more progress in securing a suitor for herself than for her cousins. *She* would be riding with Lord Wickham tomorrow, but if they so much as got walked home from church by their beaux it would be a wonder.

"You forget," Cecilia pointed out, "tomorrow afternoon Lord Wickham will not be leading your fellows astray. If their customary pastime is to traipse about after him, they will be at loose ends. I cannot believe Wickham means to bring such a retinue on our ride."

This gave sufficient encouragement that Mrs. Meacham sent out for a green goose, to be prepared in case of company.

Cecilia said, "You will be seeing the gentlemen at church tomorrow, I trust?" This was confirmed.

"Then you must encourage them to escort you home."

"Henley does bring me home—when he is there, I mean," Martha said, with an air of complaisance.

"Kind of him," Cecilia replied, trying to control a sneer. "As he is a fan of Wickham's, be sure to tell him that Wickham will be calling for me later in the day. If you can convince him I meant no slur on his tailoring, that might induce him to remain."

"He will very likely stay if Lord Wickham is coming. Nothing is more likely to make him stay," Martha said.

For the remainder of the evening they discussed arrangements for next Saturday's rout. There were to be ten couples in all, and six sets of parents. Enough to allow dancing and cards respectively. Melancholy was kept at bay by this planning, and at eleven they retired.

At church on Sunday there was a surprise in store for the village. Who should go striding down the aisle to his family pew but Lord Wickham. Every head in the place turned, and every eye stared, as though he had been a tiger on the loose. It occurred to Cecilia that his coming might have something to do with herself, but really attending church was not necessary to lend their flirtation an air of respectability. Soon her mind wandered down a different path. The Abbey was five miles from Laycombe. If he meant to call for her at three, he would have to move quickly to get home, take lunch, change, and return to the village. This was putting himself to more bother than merely dropping in while he was making a call to his solicitor!

A chat with Kate Daugherty after the service enlightened Cecilia as to how matters really stood. Lord Wickham had met her papa yesterday in the village. The vicar had done some strong hinting for a new organ, and Wickham had promised to attend a service to judge for himself whether one was required. The Daughertys had invited Wickham to take his mutton with them. He had brought his riding clothes with him and would call on Cecilia after lunch, bringing Lady with him.

While the ladies stood chatting together outside the old stone church, their gentlemen came up to join them, one by one. First came Sproule, a tall, thin, tow-haired young man. His interest in Mohammadanism never kept him from church. His own brother was in Holy Orders, and his whole family was religious. Next came Wideman. Dallan hung back a moment, perhaps because Miss Cummings was of the group. But when Lord Wickham headed toward the same party, he fell in with him and they came together to give their greetings.

Dallan bowed stiffly to Cecilia and said, "Good morning, ma'am," with only the remnants of a sneer.

The sneer soon faded when Wickham said to her, "A fine day for our ride, Miss Cummings." Dallan looked nonplussed, and turned aside to speak to Martha. He was soon complimenting Cecilia on her bonnet in a much warmer tone, and when she returned a compliment on his jacket, he began to find her a pretty good sort of woman.

"Daresay Stultz made my jacket a trifle tight about the waist," he admitted to Martha. "Mama can let it out."

A regular caravan set out for Meacham's house three blocks away. Sally Gardener took the ill-advised idea of trying to crash the charmed circle, but Mrs. Meacham diverted her to warn her she had best get a good grip on her reticule, in case she

71

should drop it. This jibe was softened by an offer of a drive home, which Mrs. Gardener accepted on behalf of herself and her daughter. At Meacham's, the group divided, with Sproule, Kate, and Wickham continuing to the vicarage. They would all return after lunch.

Dallan and Wideman accepted an offer to remain to lunch with the Meachams, and as Wickham was lost to them for a few hours, they arranged to drive out with the girls. Sproule and Kate, they were sure, would want to be of the party as well. They would all drive halfway to Tunbridge Wells and back. It sounded a flat enough outing to Cecilia, but her cousins considered it a treat of the highest order. There was much dashing talk between the gentlemen of their bits o' blood, sixteen miles an hour, and a mention of a race which would likely come to nothing, but made them feel bang up to the mark in front of Cecilia, whom Dallan now permitted to be top o' the trees.

They could not set out till Wickham had come, but as he did no more than stand at the door bowing and offering Cecilia his arm, they were soon off on their jaunt halfway to Tunbridge Wells. Mrs. Meacham whispered aside to Cecilia that she must feel free to invite Wickham back to dinner if she wished. Cecilia decided to wait till they had returned and see if the others were remaining.

Lady was a frisky, silk-mouthed filly. As there was no mounting post, Wickham had to lift her into the saddle. It was a lady's saddle, brown with blue trim. She wondered if it had belonged to his wife. "You were to alert me to her tricks," Cecilia reminded him.

She made a pretty picture, looking down on him from the horse's back, with the sun lighting her youthful face. There was health as well as beauty in her countenance and a general air of charm in her fashionable outfit. A feeling of well-being came over him, as if life might be worth living after all. Some elemental emotion had already assaulted him when he sat in the old stone church, where he had sat so many times in happier days. But that had been more nostalgic. Out in sunny nature with a pretty young escort, it felt like a new beginning. He must tread softly or he'd find himself in danger. "You must know a lady uses no tricks, ma'am," he replied lightly.

"You leave me to deduce that a gentleman does, then, as your pretext for escorting me on my first ride was to introduce me to Lady's quirks."

"Ah, a gentleman, that is another matter. We are all full of tricks," he laughed. "That is a very becoming riding habit, by the by," he added, skimming his eyes over her lithe body, that sat with natural grace on horseback.

"Thank you. Am I to assume flattery is one of the tricks I must be on guard against?"

"An Incomparable—do they still use the word?" She nodded. "An Incomparable like yourself must have received enough compliments and flattery to distinguish between them. You notice I did not compliment your bonnet. I don't care for it. It is too severe. That glowing face deserves to be surrounded by flowers."

"That is plain speaking to be sure, but for riding, flowers and feathers are a nuisance. In what direction do you mean to ride?"

Compliments and complaints, both rolled off her like water. Her obvious indifference to his opinions intrigued him. He didn't want her undying devotion, but she should be at least a little interested in his feelings. "Toward the Abbey, if you have no objection."

They cantered out through the west end of the village into a countryside brimming with golden sunlight, burgeoning with leaves and blossoms in early spring. The fresh greenery spoke of rebirth after a long, dark winter. Above them, birds soared in the azure arc of sky and chirped their mating call from every branch. They exchanged remarks on the beauty of the day, and after a mile, Wickham asked if she had yet determined the length of her stay.

With her mind half on nature, Cecilia said heedlessly, "There is no saying how long it will take— that is," she added, flustered, "I am not sure how long, as yet."

"On what does it depend, if it is not presumptuous of me to inquire?"

"Different things," she said vaguely. "I am visiting about here and there till the Season opens."

"But the Season opens next week."

"I shall not go at once if I am enjoying myself here," she said, and chatted on to distract him. "I have just come from a delightful visit with relatives in Kent. Their daughter married only last month. Before that I was with a school friend up north. She, too, married before I left."

"Marriage appears to follow hard on your heels. I wonder it has not caught up such a lovely lady before now."

A smile curved her lips, to hear the old familiar refrain. "One never knows. Marriages, they say, come in threes." Kate, Alice, and Martha, they would all have a husband soon. Lord Wickham wondered about that smile. It was not the smile of gratification at his implied compliment. What was the mys-

tery about her visit? "How long it will take ..."
That sounded as if there was one particular reason
she was here. "I don't count myself quite an old cat
yet, you know," she added.

"A mere kitten," he assured her. "One never im-
plies a single lady is anything but a girl, whatever
her age, unless she chooses to put on her caps and
set up as an acknowledged quiz. I have a chit of an
aunt in her forties who never misses a ball and still
wears pink ribbons in her hair."

"Compared to your aunt, I am a mere infant. I
wonder you mention her at all in connection with
my case," she teased.

"Age cannot be a subject for avoidance with one
so young," he assured her, but he noticed she was
tender on the subject all the same. How old was
she? Not a deb, certainly. "You cannot be more than
twenty," he said leadingly.

"Oh until she is married, a young lady never goes
past twenty," Cecilia replied lightly. "But if I were
married, I would be two and twenty. Shocking, is
it not?"

"Shocking," he agreed. "And you still ride and
dance. I expect you have a Bath chair on order,
awaiting your next birthday."

"It is not nice to tease an ape leader, sir." Cecilia
smiled and rode on. "Oh, what is that beautiful
place there on the left?" she asked later. Below
them in an emerald green valley nestled a gray
stone building—old, low, rambling. Vines climbed
up the left facade, encroaching on the leaded windows that sparkled in the sunlight. To the left, a
porte cochere arched in a graceful curve, terminat-
ing in columns. On the right, set back some distance from the main building, the relics of a ruined
chapel stood erect, with blue sky visible through

the unglazed lancet windows. A flock of pigeons, disturbed by some domestic emergency, suddenly fluttered in a silver rustle from the roofline, swooping and soaring about in the air at random before returning to their perch.

"How lovely!" she sighed. "That is what is so particularly enjoyable about riding in an unknown district. One occasionally comes across these marvelous views. What is the place called?"

"St. Martin's Abbey," he said simply, but with a trace of pride in his voice. "My place."

"I thought it was five miles away! We have not come more than three."

"It is five miles by the main road. We've taken a short cut. We can leave the road here and ride through the meadow. There's a fence ahead. Lady can take it—can you?"

With her eyes and mind full of the sight before her, Cecilia found no slight in the question, though she counted herself an excellent horsewoman. "Lead on," she said, and cantered along beside him.

"The Abbey is very old," he said. "Four hundred years old. Outside of necessary repairs and some small additions, it is not much changed from the original. Some walls had to be knocked down inside to enlarge the rooms in one wing. The monks' rooms were hardly more than closets, just space for a pallet and a prie-dieu, but that was done long before my time. From here it looks as it must have looked long ago." He reined in and they stopped to admire it.

"It is so beautiful, I wonder you could bear to stay away so long," she said softly.

"I couldn't. Not any longer, I mean. It is why I returned."

This, and your wife's death, Cecilia thought to

herself. But aloud she inquired about the extent of his lands, and he pointed into the distance, describing his acreage. She thought they might ride closer to the Abbey, but Wickham rode west, warning her of the fence to be taken. "Perhaps you would like to come with your cousin one day and look over the place," he suggested, when she was again by his side.

"I would love it of all things!" It seemed all Lord Wickham's unsociable habits were being overturned. Her triumphant smile was for this, but as he watched her, he felt a qualm of misgiving and hoped she didn't misread politeness into something else.

"Over there are some of my tenant farms," he continued, indicating a row of thatched cottages. For a man who spent his days in pleasure and his nights in dissipation, Wickham managed to keep his estate well tended. Of course a good bailiff could do that.

They rested awhile, enjoying the view. While they were still there, a farmer came pelting up behind them. With a bob of his head he said, "G'day, sir. Mum."

"Blackie," Wickham said with a smile, and talked with him a moment. Their easy conversation told Cecilia that Wickham was no stranger to his tenants. She let her mare wander a few paces away to champ the grass and could not hear their actual words, but the tone was friendly.

Soon Wickham joined her. "Blackie has discovered a barrow in the west pasture. Very fortunate! If it had been in ploughed ground, it would have been destroyed. Would you care to see it?"

His air of eagerness suggested that he wanted to go there at once himself, and she agreed. "These old barrows are some sort of burial ground from ancient days, I have heard," she said as they advanced. "Are they Roman?"

"No, they are much earlier. Neolithic, in fact. From what Blackie has described, it is a small grave, so we cannot expect a great haul. Perhaps a few flint arrowheads, a beaker if we're lucky. But there is always the possibility of a real find."

The barrow proved not very interesting. It looked like no more than a gentle swelling of the ground, about eight feet long and four wide, but after Wickham had examined it for a moment, he seemed satisfied. Blackie soon joined them, mounted on a donkey and carrying ropes, stakes, and shovels. "Will I start digging her up?" he asked hopefully.

Wickham gave him a jeering look. "On the Sabbath? It must wait till tomorrow, but you've earned your monkey today." He passed a gold coin to his tenant. That seemed to be the man's real interest, and he set about roping off the barrow for the morrow's dig. Cecilia felt it would have been done at once if she were not there.

They turned around and began to reverse their ride at a leisurely pace. "Have you found many old graves?" she asked.

"Three, thus far. Nothing very exciting, but every one adds something to our knowledge of the past. I became a little interested in archaeology—I am no expert—during my travels. Being in Italy aroused my interest as to Roman ways, and the Roman occupation of Britain, then of course I wondered what had preceded the Romans. After my return, I began to study all this more systematically. In Italy, and Greece, too, it is not uncommon for farmers to unearth real treasures while tilling the land. Unless the pieces are fully intact, they might be cast aside as rubbish, or if they're domestic vessels, they might be used in the kitchen."

"I'm surprised they would still be usable."

"They're made of clay. It doesn't deteriorate quickly. I had the most amazing experience in Italy. I stopped at a farm house for a drink near Perugia, and wine was poured from an Estruscan vase—a beautiful thing. The man told me he had dug it up in his olive orchard. I began scouting around after that and came across some few items of interest there and elsewhere. Later, near Athens some local workmen were disassembling a derelict temple and hauling away the pieces to reuse elsewhere. I managed to claim some statuary, not in the best repair, but I gathered up what bits and pieces I could find and have some hope of restoring them. My ignorance and eagerness tell me they are the work of Praxiteles, but no doubt Lord Elgin will disillusion me when he comes to view them."

These would be the 'stark naked' statues Mrs. Meacham had complained of. Cecilia was beginning to see that Wickham had been misjudged by his neighbors. He was more a scholar than a lover of statues of naked ladies. Neither did she believe his time was completely given over to amusement and dissipation. As she had no notion of revealing her former opinion of him, she said, "Let Elgin get a glimpse of them and you have lost them forever. He'll add them to his collection."

"To be fair, he gave the Elgin marbles to the British Museum."

"Beware of Elgin bearing gifts. They cost the government thirty-five thousand pounds."

"The rescue cost him more than that. He had the deuce of a time getting them home."

"I have heard that story often enough, from his own lips," she said.

"My pieces will no doubt end up in a museum as well, but I don't see that it cannot be done here, in Sussex. At the moment, I've hired artisans to try to patch them together. They're working in my barn, which don't please my shepherds. I have one nearly perfect piece, which I shall keep to myself. It's a faun, done life-size in marble. Perfect, but for the left rear foot, which is missing. I dug for days, but couldn't find it. Pity."

Wickham continued discussing his travels and his hobby in an intelligent manner, urged on by questions from Cecilia. She had not seen him so animated, so natural, and so likable before. She began to conjure again with the idea of having him replace Dallan, but felt it would require hard work on Martha's part. She would have to study up on this archaeology business to excite his interest. At the very least, he must be coerced to lessen his attentions to Dallan and Wideman.

She said, "With all your archaeological activities, I am surprised you find time to be an habitué of Jack Duck's Tavern, Wickham." During the ride he had asked her to dispense with his title.

"One cannot mope about the estate forever. Jack Duck's is a mere diversion."

"You would have me believe no one ever invites you out?" she said archly.

"They were used to, when I first returned. Taking mutton with a bunch of married folk—dull stuff."

"Surely there are some unmarried ladies in the vicinity." She was struck with the idea that if he could not care for Martha, and really she was too provincial for him, she would find a wife more in his own style. She was soon imagining a note of wistfulness in his voice when he spoke of his married neighbors. Why should he not remarry? He was still young and not the loose fish sort of gentleman she had been told. He struck her as a serious person.

"I expect so," he replied, but with no enthusiasm.

Having less wisdom than Mrs. Meacham, and more gall, she said, "You would find your neighbors less dull if you were married yourself, perhaps." She peered from the side of her eyes to see his reaction to this.

His jaw firmed to concrete. He shouldn't have shown her the Abbey. She had read too much into it. At two and twenty, she was looking for a husband, not a flirt. After a noticeable pause he said, "I have been married. Did I not tell you I was a widower?"

"Yes, but surely that does not preclude your marrying again?"

"I have no thought of marrying," he said, in a cool voice.

"A man in your position ought to think about it, Wickham. You will want a son and heir."

"I have an heir. My cousin will make a fine earl. The name and title will not vanish."

She had spoken of marriage more than once, and now this powerful persuasion. Of course a man wanted a son and heir, which required a wife. Eventually he would marry someone like Miss Cummings, someone of his own class, with more town bronze than the local girls. She was a much more attractive lady than he had planned to take as wife, but there was no reason a bride of convenience need be an antidote after all. He even admitted that she provided the sort of companionship he had been missing since his return. In time, his feeling for her might have become serious, but to have her boldly put herself forward in this manner got his back up. No, he definitely did not want a managing woman on his hands. He made it perfectly clear that he had no interest in marrying her.

Cecilia accepted her initial rebuff with good will, but persisted. "If it is only the company of married people you spurn, perhaps you will accept an invitation to a rout party of single people at my cousin's house next Saturday."

"It is very kind of you to take pity on me, but it happens I have company coming to the Abbey next weekend," he answered unhesitatingly and without apology.

This was an unpleasant jolt. Cecilia didn't consider herself a proud woman, but to have her invitation rejected so positively, without even a pretense of regret, annoyed her. "I trust your company will not include Dallan and Wideman?" Lord, the party would disintegrate before it ever began.

"No, it is friends from London," he said vaguely.

She relaxed to hear it. All was not lost then. Yet something was definitely lost. The gathering would hold nothing of special interest for herself. The happy mood had fled, as had Wickham's gallantry. They rode directly back home, with no further compliments to Cecilia. When he left her at the door, he declined a glass of wine. He didn't refer to the invitation for her to come to the abbey. Cecilia was in a fit of pique when she joined Mrs. Meacham. The others had not yet returned.

Mrs. Meacham told her the Gardeners had dropped in and asked a million questions about Lord Wickham. "It was better than a raree-show to watch them. Sally was in the boughs to see you ride off with him when she has been throwing her bonnet, as well as every parcel she carries, at him this past year. I invited them to our rout party."

"Miss Gardener will be wasting her time. Wickham has declined," Cecilia said.

"Declined? Oh dear, then our little party is all to pieces. He will haul the lads off to Jack Duck's."

"No, he has company coming from London—older company I imagine. The suitors should be safe. We must wring an acceptance out of them today."

"We'll make them stay to dinner. The green goose is roasting. Wideman loves a green goose."

"Wideman is not the real problem, ma'am. It is Dallan."

"I know it well, and he'd have preferred mutton, but we had that last Sunday and again on Wednesday."

When the suitors returned close to dinnertime, famished from the fresh air and exercise, Dallan did not refuse the invitation to sit down to dinner. And when Cecilia casually mentioned that Wickham would be busy next Saturday evening, he did not refuse the invitation to the rout either. Definite acceptances were obtained from all three gentlemen. Andy Sproule and Kate stayed to dinner as well.

Dallan even condescended to a game of jackstraws with the others in the evening. He was in good humor, and told Martha before he left that he'd drop around sometime before she left for London if he had time. He might want her to pick up something for him. With this piece of impertinence she was well pleased.

Chapter Eight

BOTH DALLAN AND WIDEMAN CAME TO CALL THE very next morning. The fact that Wickham was engaged in digging up his barrow was held to account for their alacrity. Soon a worse notion occurred to Cecilia. Wideman behaved decently. Though the younger, he was more sensible. It was Dallan whose behavior caused a spasm of alarm. Soon she understood it was herself who was the cause of this call. Intent on showing off in front of the dasher, Dallan was at his very worst. He sprawled in his chair, he assumed a bored expression, and worst of all, he fairly ignored Martha and directed what few remarks he chose to make to Cecilia. His tone implied that they two cosmopolitans were as one in disparaging provincial life.

"So you are off to London, Miss Cummings. I envy you. You must be bored to flinders here."

"Not at all. I find Laycombe very interesting."

"Just so," he said, with a jeering and conspiratorial smile that said, why else would you be leaving? "You plan to remain overnight?"

"Yes, too much of the day would be eaten up in travel if we did it in one day."

He hooked his arms over the back of his chair

and said, "My rig makes it in ninety minutes. Sixteen miles an hour. It's a consolation to know decent entertainment is close at hand."

Yet she knew perfectly well a trip to London was a great occasion for him. "I have often heard such a speed boasted of, but have never been in a rig that achieves it," she replied coolly.

"My nags do it with no trouble. Wickham's team beats even mine."

Cecilia, uncomfortable with Martha's accusing eyes on her, was lured into poor manners. "His team must be worth a fortune then, for I have not heard even the most lying braggart mention a speed *above* sixteen miles an hour."

"Well, his can do it, for he beats me in a race, and mine do sixteen."

"Indeed! Excuse me, Mr. Dallan—"

"Call me Henley."

She avoided this pitfall by not calling him anything. "I must speak to my woman about the packing," she said, and made an excuse to leave the room for a moment, so that Dallan would take the empty chair by Martha.

She returned five minutes later to find Martha, the gudgeon, had moved to sit by him. He paid her little heed, but fiddled with the ribbon of his quizzing glass, dropped it, looked at his fingernails, then finally honored Martha with a word. "You might pick me up a new snuffbox in London, Martha."

Thrilled to be recognized at last, Martha immediately expressed her delight and asked what sort of a box he would like.

"A summer box. Something light and bright. One of those with an enameled lid. Cecilia will know what they are called." He called across the room to

her, using her first name when she had not asked
him to.

"They are called cloisonné, Mr. Dallan," she replied.

He used it as an excuse to remove to a chair halfway between the two ladies. "That's it. Wickham
has one of the sort I mean, with dancing nymphs
on the lid. I'm willing to go as high as a guinea."

"I doubt you'll find a good one for that price," she
said, to deflate his pretensions.

"Two guineas then," he allowed, having no idea
what the trinket might cost, but a very good idea
that two guineas was a deal more than he cared to
spend.

"You will want to give Martha the money," she
said, as his hand remained on the arm of the chair,
fiddling endlessly with his quizzing glass. He finally drew out his purse, and Martha hopped up
like a servant to get the money. Cecilia longed to
bang their heads together. All Martha's good intentions of making Henley toe the line vanished when
she was actually with him.

"I don't want anything garish, mind," he told her.
"You'd best let Cecilia make the selection."

Martha looked like a whipped dog. It was too
much to be borne. "I doubt my taste would suit you,
Mr. Dallan, and in any case I shall be very busy,"
Cecilia said. "If you do not trust Martha's taste,
you had best execute the errand yourself."

He chose to ignore this setdown. "Coming back
Thursday, are you?" he asked. The question was
directed to Cecilia, who did no more than nod her
head.

"At what hour?"

As Cecilia turned to speak to Mrs. Meacham, it
was Martha who answered. "We will be home by

dinnertime," she said, thinking he was eager to see her.

"Good. Then I'll have my new box for Friday night. There's an Egyptian dancer coming to Jack Duck's. Famous sport. Wickham saw her in London. She wears practically nothing but gold chains and diaphanous harem pants."

Martha stuck her finger in her mouth in alarm and looked to her mentor for guidance. "There is no accounting for taste," Cecilia said, with an incredulous smile at Dallan.

The gentlemen left, after staying barely twenty minutes. Martha went to the bow window to watch the marvelous sight of their rigs driving off at an alleged sixteen miles an hour, which, strangely, did not leave any other carriages in their dust. "That was very nice of them to come to say good-bye," she said.

Cecilia could only stare. "The next time Mr. Dallan comes to make an errand runner of you, you might let him know the favor is on your side."

"But he must trust my taste, as he is letting me pick out the box by myself."

"How can he doubt it, when you've chosen him?"

"I never thought of that," the simple girl said with a smile.

Cecilia had some hopes of a call from Wickham before their departure. There was a matter of a visit to the abbey to be settled. He was seen once in the village, but he didn't call. In fact, he didn't stop at all, and Sally Gardener had the bother of flinging on her bonnet for nothing. Tuesday brought no gentleman callers, and Wednesday morning they set out early on their trip.

Once they were on the road, all thoughts were directed forward to London. The Meachams, though living so close, did not go often. When Mr. Meacham was alive, he was too busy on the estate, and after his death it seemed difficult to go without a male escort. They had at least seen St. Paul's and the Tower of London and such basic tourist spots, but wasted no time there. This being a ladies' trip, they were not obliged to appear interested in anything but shopping and visiting and enjoying themselves.

The Meachams' major acquaintance with London shopping was the Pantheon Bazaar. Cecilia directed them away from it to the more elegant establishments, where it was unclear whether it was the luxurious merchandise or the high price that left them speechless. The real reason for the trip was to line up beaux for the next assembly, and to this end they made a few house calls. Cecilia had the good fortune to find her favorite cousin, Sir Nigel Pincombe, at home and had no hesitation to open her budget to him. Besides being cousins, they were also near neighbors in Hampshire and were as close as siblings. During the visit, she got him aside for a private coze.

"What I require is bucks who make a good first impression," she told him frankly. "It matters not if they are betrothed or ramshackle or their pockets to let, so long as they can put a green light in the eyes of a pair of desultory suitors."

Sir Nigel shook his head and laughed. "Still up to your old managing tricks, Cecilia. Will I do for one beau?"

She examined him objectively. He was tall, handsome, with dark hair, and a lively nature. "You will do admirably. Two or three more as presentable as yourself is all I require. And by the by," she added with a sly look, "there is no need to advertise that we are cousins."

"Ashamed of me, are you?"

"On the contrary, you are so dashing that I may claim you for my own special beau."

"Now that is a new ploy! Don't tell me *you* have been hit with Cupid's arrow!"

"It is not a question of my actually throwing my cap at anyone. It is only that a certain lord is proving—difficult," she said, choosing her word with care. "I shouldn't mind letting him know I'm not firmly glued to the shelf."

He examined her with a disbelieving eye. "Even that is more interest than you have shown before."

"Well, perhaps he has pricked my pride," she allowed, and laughed at her own folly.

Nigel's assistance made further calls unnecessary, and the ladies had time to lavish on the selection of Dallan's snuffbox. This treat was saved for last. Cecilia's opinion was sought, and she recommended the ugliest box in the shop. It bore on its lid a nude Venus, with cupids gamboling round. She was sure Dallan would like it excessively. In the evening she took her guests to an inferior comedy at Covent Garden, which they all, including herself, enjoyed immensely.

They made another quick dash to the shops in the morning and left for Laycombe at eleven, reaching home in the early afternoon. Dallan called, as promised, on Thursday evening to pick up his snuffbox. He allowed that it was "a handsome little thing." He didn't think to thank Martha for her help in the half hour that he remained. George Wideman didn't come at all, but he had an excuse. Mrs. Gardener had told them his papa was abed with the flu, and he was kept pretty busy at home.

Wideman did make good his promise to present himself for the rout on Saturday, as did everyone else invited except Lord Wickham. Sally Gardener, having heard that he was invited but not that he declined, had a new jonquil gown made up especially for the occasion. She also came with two feathers stuck into her hair, a pair of fish-scale pearl beads down to her waist, and half a bottle of scent sprinkled over her gaunt body. The room reeked of lavender the whole night, even after Cecilia surreptitiously opened a couple of windows behind the drapes.

High spirits prevailed, especially amongst the younger set who wasted no time in electing a volunteer to play the pianoforte for them while they romped about the room. Henley Dallan danced first with Martha, then, bowing at the waist, requested the pleasure of standing up with Cecilia. She found he did not improve on longer acquaintance. The tone of his conversation was an unpleasant blend of incredible compliments and casualness that their short acquaintance did not warrant.

"It's not a bad sort of party for a change," he allowed. "I disliked to have to turn Wickham down. He's off to Jack Duck's to see the Egyptian dancer tonight."

Her ears perked up. "I understood he had company this weekend," she said.

"Ah!" He gave a knowing laugh. "Just so. I daresay he took his company to Jack Duck's."

She already suspected his company was imaginary, but she thought Wickham was at least civil enough not to broadcast his true intentions. And to have tried to lure Dallan, and likely George, too, into deserting the party riled her greatly.

"He asked you to go along with him, did he?" she asked offhandedly.

"We usually go with him" was his noncommittal reply.

"You're being evasive, Mr. Dallan."

"I wish you will call me Henley."

Even this sacrifice was made to get at the truth. "Did he ask you to go with him, Henley?"

"Certainly he asked us," he said. Not a lie in the least. "I guess you won't be going to Jack Duck's this Saturday" was an invitation. What else could you call it?

"I am happy you refused him," she said, and actually smiled at Henley Dallan. For once, she was happy with him. The words were no sooner out of her mouth than she regretted them.

"How could I go with him, when I knew *you* would be here?" he asked, eyes burning with passion, or some heated emotion. Perhaps it was only pleasure at standing up with a lady so much more stylish than the local girls.

"Of course Martha and I would be here," she said, pretending to misunderstand.

He wasn't about to let her off with that stunt. "Oh, she is always here," he said, in a swaggering way. "We were talking about us."

There was no longer any getting away from an unpleasant scene. The sooner this idea was dispelled, the better. "There is nothing between us, except that you are my cousin's special friend," she said bluntly.

He accepted it better than she hoped. A vastly superior smile, a conspiratorial wink, and an ambiguous, "Just so," that hinted at future intimacy.

Cecilia could hardly get away from him fast enough after this vexatious interlude. She was in no

91

mood for further harassment when Sally Gardener accosted her between sets.

"A pity Lord Wickham couldn't be here this evening," Sally said. For her it was not a total disaster. Though it robbed her of his company, it robbed Miss Cummings of a stellar conquest as well.

"I hope we can contrive to be merry without him."

"He seemed so particular in his attentions to you, I made sure he would be here."

"You were mistaken."

"You must not take it as a personal insult, for we who know him better know that he seldom goes into company, Miss Cummings," she explained, with a superior smile.

"I would hardly take it personally that he had to decline an invitation to my cousins' party," Cecilia pointed out.

"That is odd. Mrs. Meacham never asked him to her routs before."

"Did she not?" Cecilia said, feigning indifference. Sally continued smiling at her in a gloating manner, thinking she had put her down a peg. Pushed past endurance, she added, "As he loaned me a mare and invited us to view the abbey, she could not well omit him, could she? A pity he had company at home. I hope his absence does not quite destroy the evening for you."

Sally's black eyes snapped. She was not subtle, but she was not stupid either and realized she had been told off. "I didn't hear you had been to the abbey," she said. Her questioning look suggested it was a lie.

"Even you could not have heard it yet, for the date is still to be arranged. Shall I let you know when the event takes place?"

"*If* it takes place," Sally riposted, and walked away.

Cecilia sat berating herself for this uncustomary rudeness, cursing her temper and Lord Wickham for his duplicity.

The evening was not a total disaster, however. Kate and Alice were making strides with their beaux, and Cecilia managed to keep herself busy with other partners to avoid further doings with Dallan. The one guest who had refused was more on her mind than the couple of dozen who had come. At midnight, a sit-down supper was served in the dining room. Mrs. Meacham said to her, "It's a pity Wickham could not be here."

"Don't fret about it," Cecilia replied. "There will be a wedding for all that." She shot a meaningful glance down the table to Alice and George.

Mrs. Meacham smiled in agreement. "That there will. A match you came to make, and a match there will be."

"Perhaps two," Cecilia suggested.

Turning, she noticed that Sally Gardener stood directly behind her, with her ears on the stretch. And let us see what you make of that, my girl, she thought to herself. The snatch of conversation was forgotten in an instant by Cecilia, but it found a restless home at the bottom of Sally's heart, where it festered sorely.

Five miles away at Jack Duck's Tavern, Lord Wickham sat with a glass before him, staring into its depth with unseeing eyes. Across the room a girl—Irish he thought, with her skin tinted brown—performed an ungainly imitation of an Egyptian belly dance to some discordant tune. He was ineffably sad for her, and for himself, and for Peg, the woman who sat at his elbow, trying to cheer him up. He was generally amused by Peg. Her rough speech revealed a sharp good humor and a lively wit. Tonight he wished her at Jericho. He was only half listening to her story about some swell from the city who was trying to lure her away. His eyes flickered from group to group, all of them ramshackle people.

They were mostly young bucks, thinking themselves daring to be in this den of iniquity, drinking blue ruin and gambling more than they could afford. And the older ones were worse; at least the youngsters would grow out of it. A pair of aging gents sat across from him, men in their forties, drinking noisy toasts to a pair of trollops young enough to be their daughters. People with nothing to do—like himself. He could have gone to Mrs. Meacham's rout. At least the company would have been respectable, if dull.

"So I says to him—are you listening at all, Wickham?" He nodded to Peg. "I says to him, 'What kind of a girl do you think I am?' And he says, 'You're not a girl.' I made sure he was giving me a dig at my age, but no, he goes on to say, 'I hope I know a lady when I see one.' A fine gent he was, but married, of course. You can always spot the married ones. They have a guilty look about them, coming to a place like this. Like boys running away from school. Take you now, you'd never mistake you for a married man."

"Would you not, Peg? I was married, you know."

"Was you really, Wickham? I never knew it. Have you got any kiddies?"

"No."

"You wife's dead, is she?"

"Yes."

94

"I wager she was a grand lady. What was she like?"

"Pretty."

"It's too bad she went and died on you." She lifted her glass and drank. "You must be thinking about her tonight. You look sad. You need a drink, Wickham. Drink up, the night's young."

"But I'm not." Till that point, he had not been thinking about his wife, but Peg's words called up her image. "What was she like?" She was tall, blonde, with a face like a Grecian statue, and about as much life. He had been a fool to marry her for her beauty, but not the first young fool to make that error. Really it wasn't fair to say she had no life; that cold reserve had broken down once she met her banker, Mr. Gregory. His image was sharply etched in Wickham's brain as well. A handsome rattle, with a second-rate character and no mind worth the name.

Wickham had thought Adrianna shy at first, shy and very beautiful, like the proverbial violet blooming unseen. He had thought he would draw her out, but he'd never succeeded. Nothing worked. Not compliments, not tenderness, not patience, certainly not the irritable impatience that had finally grown in him. He often wondered if her parents had pushed the match on her. It couldn't have been for money. Her father was rich. Very likely it was the title, so overvalued by those who didn't have one. If that was the case, it was the father who aspired to a connection with the nobility. Adrianna's Mr. Gregory had no handle to his name, but she had willingly dashed off, leaving husband, home, and family to live in exile with Mr. Gregory. He hoped she had found happiness in those few years with him.

She had never looked more lovely than the night she told him she was leaving, and till that moment he hadn't realized she hated him. She had lived three years under his roof, sharing every intimacy, always with a polite facade, and all the time she had hated him. "You may sneer and look down your aristocratic nose all you like, my fine Lord Wickham, but I'd rather live in sin with Mr. Gregory if I damn my soul to eternal hellfire, than to live with you a day longer." He couldn't remember what answer he had made to that. The shock of it had probably rendered him speechless. He had a very vivid memory of her yanking off her wedding ring and hurling it at his feet. "And you can keep your precious family heirlooms, too, and your boring old abbey. I hope I never *see* another abbey."

She probably had, but she had not seen his again. Aside from the disgrace of it, he had been happy enough to be rid of her. Three years of cool politeness had cured him of any desire for marriage. Toward the end, they lived in London, sometimes not meeting for two or three days at a time. The abbey had been like a prison, with just the two of them rattling around in it, trying to keep out of each other's way. The company they invited to take the edge off their boredom hadn't helped much. Adrianna had always been ill at ease with his friends, although she seemed eager to have them come.

No trick to make her feel at home had worked. He had thought if she redecorated the place to her own taste, she might like it better. They never got past the main drawing rooms. She liked blue, had chosen blue window hangings, but there her ideas ran out. How he had come to loathe those blue hangings! Did she prefer French or English furniture? "You choose, Alfred. Your taste will be unexceptionable." In other matters, too, she was apparently without an opinion of her own. Would she like to go to Brighton for a spell, or to Scotland? "You choose, Alfred. You know those places better than I." He wondered why she had not asked him to choose her lover. A wry smile settled on his lips.

"Penny for your thoughts," Peg said, trying to cheer him up.

"That's about what they're worth."

"Ah, you're thinking of your poor wife. It's no good coming here nights to drink yourself into forgetting her. You oughta marry some nice girl and have yourself a family."

"Once was enough."

"Weren't you happy then? Didn't you love her?"

"Of course I did. You don't marry someone you don't love."

"Ha, don't you believe it! Plenty do. They marry for money. I wouldn't say no to Jack Ketch himself, if the dibs was in tune. And you a fine lord—any lady would have you."

Very likely it had been the title. Adrianna's rare shows of liveliness had centered around his titled friends. "Is he a *real* duke?" she had asked once of Beaufort. "Imagine, we had two barons and a marquis at our table!" she said another time. But the titles had not stood up to Mr. Gregory's passion in the end. "He has *feelings* and that's more than you have." Funny, he had tried to curb his passions around Adrianna. She was so cool, so collected— who would have thought she craved passion?

"Shall we have another bottle of wine?" Peg asked, forcing herself to smile, though it was midnight, and she must be dog tired. She got a commission on each bottle.

"I'm poor company tonight." He handed her a gold coin. "You have another bottle, Peg."

"Coo, it don't cost this much!"

"That's compensation for my dreary company. I'm running along now. Take care, Peg."

She slid the golden boy into her pocket and swayed over to another table, with a smile over her shoulder at Wickham.

He felt touched at that wistful smile. What a life, doomed to sit out one's every evening in this hole. It felt good to get out in the clean, cool air. It chased away the shadows of memory. He wouldn't come back to this place. It was too depressing. Dallan had introduced him to it, and in a small village there was nothing better to do. At least it provided something more than gambling.

As he rode along, cold stars twinkled overhead in an ink-black sky. Trees loomed like earth-bound clouds in the distance. It was a lonely, eerie ride, with no company to beguile the trip. His mind roved over his past life, then looked into the future. He was well to do, thirty-three years old—not too old to begin again. As Miss Cummings had so slyly pointed out, he wanted a son and heir. A pity a man couldn't buy one; it would be so much easier than saddling himself with another wife. Memories of Adrianna always turned him against another marriage. He entered Laycombe, and as he rode past Meachams', the sound of music came through the windows Cecilia had opened to dilute the fumes of Sally Gardener's scent. He took one look, then rode on without glancing behind him.

Inside, Mrs. Gardener turned to her daughter and said, "I feel a wretched wind on my back, Sal. I'm sure a window has been left open, for the curtains are blowing. Close it, will you, before I come down with a chill."

Sally slid behind the golden drapery. As she closed the window, she saw Lord Wickham's black stallion trotting down the road. She stared to confirm that she was not mistaken. She closed the window and hastened straight to Cecilia's side.

"If you care to take a look, you'll see Lord Wickham just jogging down the road—alone. It seems he didn't have company to take to Jack Duck's, after all," she said triumphantly. "I wonder why he told you he had company."

She put her hand on Cecilia's elbow to lead her to the window. Cecilia shook it off. "You must ask him, the next time he picks up your parcels, Miss Gardener."

Cecilia wouldn't lower herself to dart to the window, but she assumed that if anyone in Laycombe would recognize Wickham and his mount, it must surely be Miss Gardener. Her cheeks were flushed with annoyance, and in her breast she felt a deeper ache that she didn't care to examine.

Chapter Nine

ON SUNDAY, IT WAS A FULL WEEK SINCE CECILIA HAD laid eyes on Wickham. She thought he might be at church, since he had attended the week before. Dallan and Wideman were there, and walked home with the ladies after, but of Wickham there was neither sight nor sound. This, coming on top of the slight of not attending the rout party, began to look like willful planning to avoid her. What could account for it? Curiosity was added to piqued pride. With her mind distracted by Wickham, she had uphill work being satisfied that the matches she had come to arrange were progressing more or less satisfactorily.

Both Dallan and Wideman accepted an invitation to luncheon, and afterwards, George suggested the two couples drive out into the country.

"And of course Cecilia must accompany us," Dallan said at once. He was always trying to entice her into intimacy.

"Oh no," Cecilia said at once. "You two couples will not require a chaperon. You may chaperon each other."

"What will you do?" he persisted.

With an excellent mount awaiting her pleasure, she said that she would be riding.

"With Wickham?" Dallan asked jealously.

She squelched the urge to inform him that it was none of his business and said, "Not today." She didn't volunteer that her only companion was the groom.

Dallan left it at this, but curtailed his own outing severely. As soon as he espied Cecilia trotting through the meadow with only a groom for escort, he claimed an errand he must perform for his mother, and the two couples were home within an hour. Wideman agreed to walk over to the vicarage with Alice, but Dallan left. His "business" was to dart home and hop astride his mount, to go chasing after Cecilia. She had ridden away from the abbey that day, west of the village.

Her aim was to calm her nerves and persuade herself she cared nothing that Wickham was proving so elusive. The appearance of Dallan, alone, darting toward her was more than her spirits could stand, and she was abrupt with him.

"What are you doing here?" she asked crossly.

"I have come to keep you company. You should have told me you had no escort," he smiled.

"I wanted to be alone. I have some thinking to do."

"Two heads are better than one. Does not this thinking jag involve me?" he asked, with a knowing look.

So, he had tumbled to it that she was here to make matches. She always knew he was the sharper of the two. "Why do you think that?" she parried.

"I keep my eyes open. Shall we dismount and stroll a little?"

"You're very clever, but I think best alone, and on horseback, Mr. Dallan."

"I have asked you to call me Henley, Cecilia. You're right about the stroll. Dull stuff. There is nothing as enjoyable as a ride. Famous good sport," he smiled, refusing to take the hint.

"Where is Martha?"

"I took her home."

This being the case, Cecilia immediately claimed fatigue and headed for home to deliver Mr. Dallan into the proper hands.

"I wish you would share with me what is troubling you," he said.

"It is a personal matter."

"I am a bit of dab at handling personal problems," he persisted.

"So am I. I can manage it, thank you."

She quickly changed the subject to a discussion of the scenery, and got him back to Meachams' house as fast as she could. Still her vexations were not over. He refused to come in. "For I told Martha I had an errand to perform for Papa. I hope you will not tell her otherwise."

"You ought not to ask me to lie to my cousin," she pointed out stiffly, though she was not eager to tell Martha the truth.

"All's fair in love and war." At least he spoke of loving Martha. That was something! "Anyway, it's not exactly a lie. I am going to call on Aunt Percival immediately." He apparently read agreement to the subterfuge in his companion's face, for he said no more about it. Before leaving, he asked, "Will you be attending the assembly on Saturday evening, Cecilia?"

"Yes, we plan to attend. Will you and Mr. Wideman be there?"

"If you are to be there, wild horses would not keep me away." This was accompanied by a soulful look from his black eyes.

She noticed the subtle shift from "You and Mr. Wideman" to "I," but ignored it. What she would have liked very much to discover was whether Wickham would be with him and sought to find out by indirection. "You won't let Lord Wickham lure you off to Jack Duck's?" she said, smiling to remove any idea of her real concern.

"I'm flattered at your eagerness. I will be there, have no fear." He bowed and got away before she could think of any way to depress his presumption or discover whether Wickham would be at the assembly.

Cecilia wore a scowl when she entered the house. It did not lessen to see Sally Gardener installed with Martha in the window seats, smirking like a pampered cat.

"So this was Mr. Dallan's errand!" she crowed. "That was a sly trick to serve your cousin, Miss Cummings." Martha cast a suspicious glance on her cousin, but said nothing.

Cecilia took a deep breath to calm her nerves and replied, "It was no trick, Miss Gardener. I met Mr. Dallan on his way to visit his Uncle Percival. He rode along this far with me."

"The Percivals live in quite the other direction," Miss Gardener announced in a voice of triumphant malice. "We have caught you out there, Miss Cummings."

"Do they, indeed? Then I must conclude Mr. Dallan's manners are exquisite, if he has gone so far out of his way to accommodate Martha's cousin."

This explanation satisfied Martha, and her next business was to ask what Henley had said.

"He made me promise to deliver you to the assembly next Saturday," Cecilia told her, with a twinge for the lie. Martha's satisfaction soared to pleasure, and she gave a sniff in Sally Gardener's direction.

"I don't suppose Henley happened to say where Lord Wickham is today?" Miss Gardener inquired.

"I didn't ask," Cecilia said loftily. She left before any further impertinences could be offered.

"You will have to keep a sharp eye on that one," Sally said, as soon as she was again alone with Martha. "Having lost out on Lord Wickham, she has set her bonnet at Henley."

"You are mistaken, Sally. My cousin does not care overly much for Henley. They are always coming to cuffs."

"What better way to draw his attention, goose?"

"No, truly. She even thinks I might look higher myself. And if she does not think him quite good enough for me, you may be sure she would not want him for herself."

"What a sly creature she is! First she tries to set your jaw against him, then she wins his attention by these flirtatious little quarrels."

"You misunderstand the matter entirely. I am quite sure it is Wickham she favors."

"Is that what she says?" Sally asked eagerly.

"Indeed no! She has not said anything of the sort, but she—she seems to like him. She is a little excited and nervous when he is coming to call, you know. And though she tried to hide it, I think she was disappointed that he didn't come to the rout last night. You may be sure that if Cousin Cecilia ever accepts an offer, it will be from an older, titled gentleman like Lord Wickham."

"How old is she?"

"In her early twenties."

"That old! She's not finding easy work of nabbing Wickham's title in any case," Sally said, and had to be satisfied with that.

Sally Gardener didn't happen to be on watch at her window when Lord Wickham arrived at Mrs. Meacham's door the next afternoon. She missed his entrance, but by the time he left, she had been summoned by her mama, who was nearly as interested in the doings of Miss Cummings and Lord Wickham as her daughter.

The Meacham girls were out on Monday afternoon when he called. They were at the vicarage making plans for a birthday party for Kate. It was their hope that their beaux could be coerced into attending. Cecilia was upstairs with the servants, making arrangements for the weekend visitors. When Miss Miser came to fetch her, Cecilia felt an unaccustomed confusion. Her fingers flew to her head to arrange her hair. She darted to the mirror and saw the bloom of a flush on her cheeks and the sparkle in her eyes. "Tell Lord Wickham I shall be down presently," she said, trying to appear calm.

"I'll make an excuse downstairs myself, to get a look at him," Miss Miser said roguishly. "You don't usually show any discomposure when a gentleman calls on you. This one must be something out of the ordinary."

"So he is, extraordinarily troublesome!" Cecilia said. "He is the one holding up my marital arrangements for my cousins."

Miss Miser, long her mistress's confidante, was not deceived by this transparent subterfuge and suggested a quick brush be taken to Miss Cummings's curls before she go down. Cecilia used the interval to determine what tack she should take

105

with Wickham. A direct confrontation was not her intention, yet she wanted to mention the rout party, and his attempt to keep Dallan and Wideman from it.

She had wiped all traces of excitement from her expression when she entered the Gold Saloon. He smile was no more than polite, and her curtsy, though graceful, was small. "Good afternoon, Wickham," she said. He rose, he bowed, with a similar sort of smile. Each made a quick survey of the other, and the smiles broadened spontaneously.

There was no denying Miss Cummings was a very handsome lady. Wickham found her something quite out of the ordinary, especially in a quiet backwater like Laycombe. Her becoming tousle of black curls, her wide-set gray eyes and her rosebud complexion were even more admired than her elegant toilette. Cecilia was measuring her caller against the ton, but still found him to pass muster.

"I expect you have come to check up on the mount you lent me," she said. "Fear not, she is unharmed and very much appreciated. I had her out for exercise yesterday and shall do the same later today."

"I'm happy you're enjoying Lady, but my reason for calling is not so innocent," he warned her. "If you have a few moments free, perhaps you would come out for a drive with me."

This suited Cecilia perfectly, as conversation in front of Mrs. Meacham was a little circumscribed. "Very well. It's too fine a day to remain indoors. I shall just get my bonnet and pelisse."

Before long, they were installed in his carriage, while Sally squinted through the curtains, taking in every detail of the affair. The only item for conjecture was that they drove not toward St. Martin's Abbey, but away from it.

"What is it you wish to discuss?" Cecilia asked, as they clipped along the High Street.

"I have come to ask you a favor, ma'am. I need your help."

"I'm very happy to give it. What can I do for you?"

He slanted a smile at her. "You are impetuous, Miss Cummings. You agree to help me before you hear what I have to say."

"Impetuosity is one of my little faults. I cannot believe, however, that you will ask anything of me that I might not with propriety grant."

"That is a pretty compliment to me. I hope the favor does nothing to change your opinion. The thing is, I am in a bind. You recall I mentioned Elgin and some fellows from the British Museum were coming down to have a look at my bits and pieces from abroad."

"Yes, and Elgin will try to get them away. Do you wish me to hide them?" she asked, her smile making it a joke.

"He'll get only what I decide to give. I want to ask you to help me entertain him and his wife. A few of the other gentlemen are also bringing their ladies. I must do something in a social way, a dinner party at least. I know of no one who would make such a charming hostess as yourself."

She looked at him in alarm. "That is a singular honor, sir. I am not at all sure I can accept."

"You misunderstand me," he hurried on. "Naturally I meant that your hostess should also be of the party, and your cousins, too. Mrs. Meacham would be the nominal hostess, but as you are acquainted with the Elgins and more familiar with entertaining on a larger scale than provincial dos, I hoped you would agree to help."

107

Put in this light, the invitation appealed to her. "I should be happy to do it, but I must first discuss it with Mrs. Meacham."

He gave her a conning smile. "There's no hope for reprieve there. I've done my reconnaissance work. She has already consented, depending on your lending a hand."

"When are your guests expected?"

"They come Wednesday afternoon and leave Thursday. It's only a brief visit, as Lord Elgin's schedule is busy. One dinner party is really all the trouble I would put you to."

"Did you want us to arrange the party—"

"No, no. I would not impose so strenuously on your good nature. My housekeeper will attend to the details. It is just your presence that I am asking."

"That is hardly a favor at all, Wickham. I will be more than happy to attend."

They left the town and drove into the open country, with a sun-drenched vista of valley beyond. Cecilia was happy with the projected party and decided to put the drive to use. "It is your being a bachelor that puts you in this awkward position," she pointed out. Oh yes, this man definitely needed a wife, and while she could not think offhand of anyone to fill the bill, she would give it consideration. A smile of anticipation lit her eyes.

Wickham took a sharp breath but said nothing. She wasn't hiding her claws! Say that for her, she was as bold as brass. "But it is only a hostess for my party that I am looking for," he said, rather pointedly.

"I did not mistake the invitation for an offer of marriage, sir!" she said, and gurgled quite delightfully, while batting her long lashes at him.

Wickham was seized with a strange compulsion to grab her into his arms and kiss those laughing lips—but he felt no desire at all to marry her. Beauty had seduced him once. If he ever married again, it would be a sensible, coolly thought-out marriage to some lady young enough to give him a son, and old and plain enough that she would never touch his heart.

As they drove on, Cecilia remembered that Wednesday was Kate Daugherty's birthday, and Martha and Alice would be attending it. She was to have attended as well, and dreaded it, as it left her prey to Dallan's advances. Wickham's dinner party made an unexceptionable excuse to miss the party. Looking at her, Wickham wondered at that pensive look. He hesitated to use the word "scheming," but "sly" seemed not too strong. Now what plan was she hatching? Her next remark seemed innocent enough.

"What did you find in the barrow Blackie discovered last Sunday, Wickham?"

"Nothing unusual. There were bones, a few flints."

"No beaker?"

"No, it was a very minor discovery. The size of the mound hadn't raised my hopes to any Olympian heights."

"A neighbor of mine found a metal knife blade in one of those old barrows. He seemed to think it a great thing. He had not thought the working of metal was known in England so long ago."

"It might have been brought from elsewhere in a trading vessel. Metalworking was certainly known in Mesopotamia. Or perhaps even in England. Very little has been done in that area. We have very little notion of our ancient past. Stonehenge, Avebury . . .''

"Oh, Stonehenge! I feel the hair on my neck lift when I stand, gazing up at those monoliths."

"You've been there?"

"Several times. I have relatives living nearby and always visit Stonehenge. Such a mystery. Who could have built it, and why?"

"People have been wondering that forever. It has been mentioned in ancient writings since the sixth century. Some credit Merlin with the miracle, but of course it doesn't feature in the King Arthur legend at all, so I think we can dispense with that theory. John Aubrey was probably closer to it. He believed the stones are the remains of a Druid temple."

"They do remind one of a primitive temple," she agreed.

"Doctor Stukely supported the notion. Others, notably Dr. John Smith, believe it has some astrological meaning."

Cecilia had some interest in the ancient monument, and as Wickham had studied the literature, they passed a pleasant half hour discussing it. They were both surprised when the town of Reigate suddenly loomed before them, and they realized they had driven farther than they intended.

As they were getting along so well, Cecilia decided to tease him about missing the rout, and more particularly about trying to lure Dallan away.

"You missed a very nice party last Saturday, Wickham. It is a pity you couldn't attend." Her knowing smile told him she suspected at least some part of the truth.

"I could have, actually," he admitted. "My company was delayed. Elgin hoped to get down on Sat-

110

urday, but he wrote at the last minute and put it off." No trace of blush suffused his face at this polite lie.

"Why did you not come to our rout then?"

"As I had already refused, I was afraid I would throw out your numbers."

"Good gracious, we aren't so formal as that! You did not fear that luring Mr. Dallan away from us would also throw out our numbers?" she added with a sapient look.

"Lure him away?" He seemed genuinely confused. "I may have mentioned why I was not attending, but I didn't attempt to lure him away, I promise you. In fact, I'm sorry I missed the party. Jack Duck's place is becoming a bore. I don't plan to return there."

Cecilia drew a breath of relief and honored him with a warm smile. "Good! I am happy to hear it. No doubt it would do an older man in your position no harm, but to take youngsters there . . ."

"I did not 'take' anyone there, Miss Cummings. Your cousins' beaux introduced me to the place. *Faute de mieux,* I accompanied them a few times. No more."

Cecilia considered this and thought perhaps he was telling the truth. Mr. Dallan at least had his own way of perceiving the world and had likely exaggerated to give the ladies the notion he was closer to Wickham than he actually was. "You stand very high in their estimation, if I am not mistaken. A word against the place from you will make them realize it is beneath them."

"Then I am happy to be able to return the kind favor you do me in hostessing my party."

Sally Gardener was highly vexed to see the bright smiles on both their faces when he accompanied Ce-

cilia to her front door. The girls had still not returned, and it was only Mrs. Meacham who sat at
the bow window, monitoring the High Street. Cecilia joined her, but before she could discuss her
drive, Mrs. Meacham peered through the curtain
and said, "There goes Sally Gardener on the run,
tying up her bonnet as she goes. Lord Wickham
must be taking a stroll down the High Street. Yes,
there he goes into the bank. What has Sally found
to throw at his feet today? She will have to make
do with her reticule, for she didn't take time to grab
up a bag from her house. A good thing it is patent
leather; she can wipe the dust from it. There! She
has dropped it smack in his path. I wonder what he
says, that she smiles so."

The conversation that could only be seen, would
have raised Miss Cummings's hackles very high,
had she heard.

"So kind. Thank you very much, Lord Wickham.
A lovely day, is it not?"

"We'll have rain before nightfall, I think."

"Very likely. It is really quite a raw, windy day.
Do you go to the bank? That is a coincidence. I am
just on my way there on an errand for Mama."

"Then you must allow me to accompany you."

"We were sorry you could not attend Mrs. Meacham's rout party. A certain young lady was very
disappointed," she said, with a sly look.

"Indeed."

"Miss Cummings was completely out of sorts that
you refused her invitation."

"I was sorry to have to do so." Pest of a woman!
He held the bank door for her and she sidled in past
him, still talking. He'd have to let her do her business first. She'd drop her pennies and shillings all
over the floor for him to pick up.

"They all had the notion that you refused their invitation only to go to the tavern," Sally continued, in no low voice. "Especially when Miss Cummings spied you riding down High Street at midnight. Very upset, she was. 'Don't think Lord Wickham will tumble into the first trap set for him,' I told her. 'He won't be that easy to catch,' I said, right to her face. She didn't know which way to look."

Wickham glared at her with a set look about the jaw, undecided whether to turn his back on the loose-jawed commoner or give her a setdown. "I'm afraid you mistake the matter," he said in a glacial tone.

"There is no mistake about it, milord," she continued happily. "Miss Cummings has come here to make a match. It is discussed quite openly— amongst the family, I mean. I daresay I was not supposed to overhear. 'A pity Lord Wickham could not be here,' Mrs. Meacham said. And Miss Cummings replied, 'Never fear, there will be a wedding soon, despite his not coming tonight.' I very nearly fell off my chair to hear her speak so blunt. Lord Wickham should be warned, I thought, and so I just dropped you a hint."

Why not a hint? She had dropped everything else. "I am obliged to you, ma'am," he said, then strode with a stiff leg to the clerk and let Miss Gardener wait behind him, to pick up her own silver when it fell from her fingers.

His mind was alive with conjecture when he went back to his carriage. Openly bruiting about that she meant to catch him, was she? And he falling into her trap, as meekly as a lamb. She hadn't even put herself to the bother of inventing a new trick to first capture his attention, but had dropped a box of buttons, like a Sally Gardener. He regretted having asked her to hostess his party, but really he required some lady, and who else was there, without putting one of the Lowreys, fifteen miles away, to the bother? He could hardly rescind the invitation already issued, but that would be the end of it. Miss Cummings would find he was not so easily caught as that.

Chapter Ten

IT WAS NO NEW EXPERIENCE FOR LORD WICKHAM TO have a bonnet hurled at his eligible head. He had become quite adept at dodging them. He felt no real danger from Miss Cummings, though she was certainly a deal prettier than most of his flirts, and a deal slier, too. He must tread softly, or he'd find himself compromised. The danger lent a spice to the affair. One dinner party was hardly apt to find him shackled, however, and he looked forward to it with some eagerness.

The day finally arrived, the company reached St. Martin's on schedule, and at six o'clock, Mrs. Meacham and Miss Cummings were admitted by the butler. The guests were abovestairs making their toilettes for dinner, and Wickham was belowstairs to greet them. Mrs. Meacham was on nettles to find herself amidst such smart society, but he noticed that Miss Cummings was no more than pleasantly eager.

"How lovely the abbey is," was Cecilia's first remark, after being greeted. The entrance retained some of its severe, ecclesiastical character. In an embrasure where once had stood a Christian effigy, there was a marble bust of some ancient Greek god or Roman emperor. This, she assumed, was one of Wickham's archaeological finds. To her left, the doorway showed a handsome saloon bathed in the light of the setting sun. Elegant striped sofas, the gleam of polished mahogany, and the glitter of sun on brass appointments gave the room an air of fashionable prosperity.

Wine was served, and before much could be said, the guests joined them. Wickham noticed that Miss Cummings was not only known to most of them, but greeted with enthusiasm.

"So this is where you are hiding yourself," Lady Elgin smiled. "I wondered that I have not seen you about town, Cecilia. Everyone has been asking for you. Your mama is not in town yet either. I shall be calling on her as soon as she arrives. Come and sit beside me and I shall tell you all the *on-dits* about your beaux. You will be coming to town for the Season, of course."

"Indeed I shall, ma'am. I am looking forward to it."

Sir Giles Middleton and his lady had to borrow her for a little catching up on gossip, and even Mr. Harpur, a studious antiquarian from the British Museum, said he was happy to see her looking so well.

Till dinnertime, there was no discussion of the marble antiquities at all. It was Wickham, and of course Mrs. Meacham, who felt like outsiders as the others spoke of the new crop of debs, of weddings and house parties, and other social matters. When they trouped into dinner, Lord Elgin rushed to partner Cecilia. Over the soup, he told her in a loud voice, "You must charm that statue of a grace out of Wickham for me, my dear. I don't know how I came to miss it at the Erechtheum. It belongs with the Elgin marbles certainly. I shan't be happy till I have it."

"You know I would if I could, but you must not imagine I have that sort of power over Wickham. We are only new acquaintances."

With a laughing look from one to the other, Elgin said, "No doubt that is why you are invited to greet his guests. Fear not, I shan't tease him, but I get a whiff of April and May here, do I not?"

"Only April, sir, and that whiff comes from the garden, no doubt."

"Very well, I shan't say a word till you are ready to make the announcement. You have chosen well, Miss Cummings. You are the very one to get Wickham back to town, where he belongs. We could have used a few influential gentlemen interested in antiquities when we were fighting Parliament for money to buy the marbles. The Philistines rule the roost there."

Wickham couldn't overhear all the conversation, but he got the gist of it and was satisfied to hear Miss Cummings assert the absence of any romance between them, even if Elgin didn't believe her. No doubt Sally Gardener had led him astray. She was a byword for gossip mongering. He also denied the charge of courting Miss Cummings when Lady Middleton teased him on the same score.

"For shame, Wickham," she said, cuffing his wrist. "Why are you dallying? Someone else will steal her away from you if you don't look lively. Miss Cummings is extremely eligible, you must know. A lovely gel."

It seemed the general consensus. All of London loved Miss Cummings, which made it unlikely she'd come to the country to find a beau. Wickham was struck by the universal approval of the notion of their being romantically involved. As he thought about it, it seemed odd that everyone should have made that assumption. It soon occurred to him that Miss Cummings might have set the notion afoot herself, to put some subtle pressure on him. The idea of inviting her here was his own; he could not lay that in her dish, but she was clever and might have decided to put the evening to use.

He made some subtle effort to discover this when the ladies went to the saloon after dinner, and the gentlemen remained behind with their port and cheroots. Finding an opening was the easiest thing in the world, for his guests seemed more interested in Miss Cummings than in his marbles.

"Are you making a match with Miss Cummings?" Lord Elgin asked him point blank.

"No, in fact, we are no more than acquaintances. It is her cousin, Mrs. Meacham, who is my friend." This evasive tactic lent a slight hue of pink to his cheeks, which Lord Elgin interpreted as he wished.

"Ha ha, I cannot imagine what the secret can be, unless you are afraid all of London's bachelors will come crashing down on your head to interfere with the match. There will be cracked hearts aplenty if you nab her. But I shan't say a word. You may rely on my silence."

"I would appreciate it, as there is really nothing to tell. Where did you get such an idea?" He waited to hear if Miss Cummings had done anything to instigate or support it.

"I have the use of my eyes. How could any man resist her? If the idea has not occurred to you, then let me put the bee in your bonnet. You could not do better than marry Miss Cummings. It would be a double benefit in that she would bring you to London, I make no doubt, and you would keep her there instead of running around the country, looking to make a match. She is away too much." This was a reference to her matchmaking tendency for others, but Wickham frowned in confusion and quickly quit the subject. He could find no hard evidence that Miss Cummings had willfully set the idea afoot.

When the gentlemen went to the saloon, Lady Middleton asked Miss Cummings to play for them. The gentlemen took up the cry, and Cecilia agreed without demur, providing Lady Middleton would honor them with a song. It was at the piano player that Wickham gazed during the concert. Miss Cummings was a talented amateur. She played with charm and liveliness, and looked exceedingly pretty with her raven head bent over the keys. He already knew her to be pretty. He had heard this evening that she was also rich. He could see she was easy in conversation with sensible people, and now he saw that she had other accomplishments as well.

When his natural partiality was added to this list, Wickham began to think Lord Elgin might be right, and she would make him a very good wife. He wondered why she had sat on the shelf so long, why it should be necessary for her to jaunter around the whole countryside, looking for a match. There must be something amiss with the girl. An unsteadiness of character seemed the likeliest thing. She could not settle down to one gentleman. That, of all faults, was the worst one for a man in Wickham's position to consider. To be jilted by your own wife once was a grave misfortune. To be so treated twice would turn the tragedy to farce. But Miss Cummings was too worldly to actually jilt her husband. She would conduct her affaires with discretion. Strangely, this idea was equally repellent, though, he certainly thought in terms of taking a mistress himself.

119

After the concert there was some general conversation. The tea was brought in and soon the party was over. It was deemed to have been a success, and Wickham accompanied Mrs. Meacham and her niece to the door, reiterating his thanks.

"I thought we would get a look at your marbles," Mrs. Meacham mentioned.

"I expect your guests spent the afternoon conning them?" Cecilia said. "I would have liked to see them, too."

"Then you must return tomorrow and see them at your leisure," he said. The offer seemed unavoidable. "My guests must leave in the morning. Come early and stay to tea. Perhaps your daughters would like to come as well, ma'am?" he suggested to Mrs. Meacham, making it a safe, family party.

She knew her girls had about as much interest in a set of busted statues as they had in politics, but they would like to see the abbey. "That would be delightful!"

"I shall look for you around two, then."

He shook their hands, thanked them once again, and they were off.

As the carriage took them home, Mrs. Meacham drew a great sigh of relief and said, "That wasn't so bad as I feared. I don't think I quite disgraced myself as Lord Wickham's hostess."

"You did admirably, Cousin."

"And tomorrow will be much easier, with only ourselves there. I cannot believe Lord Wickham is as rackety as we thought. Surely Lord Elgin is top of the trees, and the Middletons are related to a bishop."

"I believe we judged him harshly. He has promised me he will not go to Jack Duck's in the future."

"Well now! It seems you have great influence in that corner, Cecilia. Lady Elgin speaks of a match between the pair of you, but I told her it is no such thing. He has not spoken to you . . . ?"

"Certainly not." Cecilia hurried on to wonder how the girls were enjoying Kate Daugherty's birthday party and by that simple ploy directed the conversation away from Wickham and herself.

Great news awaited them when they reached home. Kate had received an offer from Andy Sproule. The wedding date was set for June.

Happy as Alice was for her friend, it soon came out that the gleam in her eye had another cause. "George said, 'I don't know what we are waiting for. I am a year older than Andy. Must we wait till Martha goes before we are shackled?' I don't see why we should." With that unromantical proposal she was *aux anges*. "He will be speaking to you soon, Mama. Must I wait for Martha?"

The only sad face in the room was Martha's. Henley had said nothing of any account, except to ask half a dozen times why Cecilia had not come.

"It seems hard for Alice to have to wait . . . I wonder if this will nudge Henley into a proposal," Mrs. Meacham said, slanting a curious eye at her elder daughter, who immediately burst into tears and fled to her room.

"It will, eventually," Cecilia prophesied. "With both Andy and George out of circulation, he will soon find himself lonesome."

"And now that Lord Wickham has promised not to go to Jack Duck's, he shan't have that diversion. I expect I shall see both my daughters bounced off before you leave, Cecilia, or at least promised."

"The company we have coming for the assembly Saturday evening might hasten the offer. We shall

121

make Martha the belle of the ball. That will open Dallan's eyes. He always likes to be in fashion, and if London beaux favor Martha, he will realize she is worth catching."

"You really are a wizard!" Mrs. Meacham declared, and kissed her a resounding smack on the cheek.

"We shan't wait past the end of summer," Alice declared. "If she can't bring Henley up to the mark by then, I will marry George."

"I doubt it will take that long," Cecilia assured her. "But are you quite sure, ma'am, that he is a suitable parti for Martha? Do you not find him a trifle unsteady?"

"It is just a phase he is going through," Mrs. Meacham told her. "He used to be better behaved, and he will be better again once he gets over this notion of being a fashionable buck. There was never anyone else for Martha. Henry wanted it, you know. If she can get him, they will have my blessing, and so will you, Cousin."

Cecilia already knew Martha to be determined in her quest, and if Mrs. Meacham thought it would do, she decided that those most intimately involved knew best. She would arrange the match if she could. She had arranged more difficult ones in the past.

It had been a full evening, and after much discussion of both parties over cocoa, the ladies went to bed. Cecilia's plans were proceeding excellently. There was not a reason in the world to be feeling so flat. What could cause it? Was it the repeated wish of all her friends at the party that she should finally be settling down? They seemed quite concerned for her. If she left off marriage much longer, folks would begin calling her a spinster. Well, Dallan already had.

She had not found the arrangement of her cousins' matches so enjoyable as usual. She would like to have blamed Wickham, but as she considered it, she admitted that any enjoyment in the affair had centered around him. Lady Elgin had hinted that he would make her an excellent parti. She had not a doubt in the world that she could have him if she wished. Without even trying, she had got farther than any of the other ladies who lived nearby and had constant access to him. Was it time to give off helping others and help herself?

She would observe Wickham carefully tomorrow and see if she could be happy with him for a lifetime.

Chapter Eleven

IT IS NOT TO BE IMAGINED THAT KATE DAUGHERTY
stayed away from Laycombe the next morning. She
spent an hour at the Meachams receiving their congratulations, expressing openly her own delight at
having got her offer from Andy, and making plans
for the wedding. Nor did she forget to tender a shy
thank you to Cecilia, whom she felt had been a
great help to her. When Sally Gardener issued from
her house, the girls took the idea of telling her and
any other neighbors who happened to be out the
great news. They put on their bonnets and went
into the street. Cecilia remained behind, congratu-
lating herself on Kate's betrothal, and planning
how to help her cousins to the same condition.

The pleasure of a trip to St. Martin's was out-
shone by Kate's visit, but it was by no means de-
spised. The carriage was brought around at one
thirty, and at the appointed hour, it drew up in
front of the abbey. Mrs. Meacham now felt quite at
home amidst the grandeur and smiled her friendly
smile at their host.

"G'day, Lord Wickham. Here we are as we promised. A dab of culture will do these hussies no
harm," she told him. "If they know a Greek from a

Roman, it is more than I do, but what we are all eager to see your broken statues. Not the naked ones, mind."

Cecilia bit back a smile at this lowly description of the artworks and went with the others to view those pieces deemed fit for the eyes of virgins and widows. She could discern little difference between the Grecian originals and what Wickham called the "inferior" Roman imitations, but at least she was interested to learn, which was more than could be said of the others. Their only wonder at the exhibition was that anyone would bother bringing home such rubble, when the monument maker at Reigate could fashion a new piece at a very good price. The angel with spread wings guarding Mr. Meacham's grave—now that was a statue!

After the viewing, Wickham showed them around some of the drawing rooms and the gallery of the abbey. When tea was served at last, the company felt completely at ease. Mrs. Meacham recognized Wedgewood china when she saw it and could venture an opinion of a fairy cake as well as the next one. She declined the offer to pour tea, passing the honor onto Cecilia. "For I am all thumbs, Lord Wickham. I would not like to spill tea on your nice carpets."

While Cecilia poured, Mrs. Meacham took note of the room's decor, deducing from it that Wickham was too nice to think the room needed redoing. She told him so in a chatty way, like a friend. While all this was going forth, Wickham watched Miss Cummings with a wary eye, imagining her at the head of his table, where he decided she would do very well.

Cecilia noticed he was observing her with unusual diligence. She already felt a little ill at ease as a result of her own thinking, and his observation added to it. It almost seemed he had read her mind and was measuring her as she measured him, in the role of prospective spouse. Confusion lent a touch of consciousness to her usually calm behavior. She found herself speaking in awkward blurts.

"The abbey is charming, Wickham. Anyone must be happy here." Then, deciding that this hinted at self-interest, she quickly added, "For a country place, I mean. For myself, I always spend part of the year in London." That was even worse, putting herself firmly at the center of it all. "Do you have a house in town?" she asked.

"Yes, I, too, spend the Season in London. I did not do so last year, so soon after my late wife's death. There was much to see to about the estate after my trip as well, but I plan to in the future, certainly."

"Lord Elgin mentioned that he would be happy to see you there, to bolster his own antiquarian interests." This hinted at having discussed him behind his back and turned her cheeks a becoming rose.

"I expect you will be leaving Laycombe soon, as the Season opens next week" was his next speech.

Even these harmless words she managed to endow with ambiguity. "I have not set a firm date. Do you go next week?" Now why had she added that pointed question, as though planning to match her departure to his?

"Soon, I have not decided precisely when I shall leave."

"Perhaps we shall meet there," she said, and gave up any hope of appearing disinterested. She was amazed at her own clumsiness. If Wickham had not guessed at her interest before now, this must surely have done it. "At parties, I mean," she added in desperation, and was unhappy with that chilly speech, too.

"I hope I may do myself the honor of calling on you," he said, smiling at her every gaucherie.

"Papa's house is in Hanover Square," she said, and took a slice of plum cake, which she did not want in the least, but would keep her mouth busy and out of mischief.

No one else noticed anything amiss in the conversation, but Wickham was surprised at her confusion. After some talk of yesterday's party, Cecilia said, "Oh, we have not seen the faun, Wickham. You mentioned it as a particularly well-preserved piece. May we see it?"

"Certainly. It is hiding from Elgin in a corner of the rose garden, behind the house. We'll just wait till everyone is finished tea."

Mrs. Meacham was far from finished. She had not even tried the plum cake and had seen quite enough marble rubble in any case. "You run along, Cousin. I am quite satisfied here."

Cecilia looked expectantly at the sisters. "Girls?"

They were disinterested in this plan, and it was only Wickham and Cecilia who left. He led her through the house, into a rose garden hedged in yews. The faun was as he had described, a lovely piece in yellowish marble, with some veining on the back that gave a suggestion of a faun's spots. "This is lovely!" she exclaimed. "It looks so natural, so perfectly at home here, as if it might lift its head and shyly dart away."

He smiled in pleasure, and said, "I have had the same feeling about you today, Miss Cummings—Cecilia. May I call you Cecilia?" His voice was soft, with an unusual warmth.

She nodded, but kept her face averted, ostensibly admiring the statue.

"Are you not going to ask me my meaning?" he prodded. She looked over her shoulder, waiting, and he continued. "You, too, look perfectly at home here, but I have had some impression of—uneasiness in your attitude. I hope you don't mean to dart away too soon."

She chose to ignore any special significance and replied, "It is time we should be leaving. The sun is beginning to lower."

He examined the sky and then drew out his watch. "It is only four o'clock! And you have all of five miles to go. That won't do for an excuse."

"We were invited to see your statues and have tea. We have done both."

"Is that the only reason I asked you?" he said archly.

Cecilia found herself more at ease in an outright flirtation than in the strained atmosphere that had formerly prevailed. "That was the reason you gave, sir, and I took you at your word," she smiled pertly.

"No fear of an ulterior motive?"

"I doubt you would have invited the family had you planned to turn into a flirt. This exercise must therefore be spontaneous."

"So it is. As to asking the family, I doubt you would have come without them. I sometimes find myself carried away when I am alone with a pretty lady."

"Forewarned is forearmed. I shall take care we are not often alone."

He walked closer, not touching her, but close enough to touch. "Now you put me in a quandary, Cecilia. I had hoped to induce you to ride out with

128

me tomorrow. We must not rob Lady of her exercise. Can you trust me to behave?"

"I have not seen anything to suggest you will not. I am free in the morning, but will be busy preparing for company in the afternoon. Guests are coming," she said vaguely. "Are you free in the morning?"

"Is ten o'clock too early? It's not the rush of business that leads me to suggest an early hour, but eagerness. I am free all morning."

"I'm an early riser. Ten is fine."

He took her arm and led her inside. After another cup of tea, the ladies rose, expressed their thanks, and left. Wickham walked with them to their carriage.

"That was just dandy, Lord Wickham," Mrs. Meacham assured him two or three times.

He nodded and smiled. "I shall see you at ten tomorrow, Cecilia," he reminded her, as he closed the door behind her.

This had to be explained as soon as the carriage was moving. "An appointment with Wickham tomorrow?" Mrs. Meacham said, surprised.

"He called you Cecilia," Alice said.

"Upon my word, I smell a match here! Don't try to tell me otherwise. I knew how it would be as soon as he laid an eye on you," Mrs. Meacham exclaimed, and laughed heartily while Cecilia disclaimed with equal vigor.

Martha gave a sulky look and said nothing. The higher Cecilia rose in everyone else's estimation, the more neglected she felt. It seemed Cousin Cecilia could arrange a match for everyone else but her. If she weren't so busy flirting with Wickham, she could do what she came to do.

* * *

Wickham called the next morning as planned, and Cecilia had herself under sufficient control that she could greet him without blushing. Her mind was pretty well made up to have him. At least she would not say no; she would ask for time to consider it. He seemed partial to her; he was eligible, and she was ready to marry. Nothing stood in the way. Upon first seeing him in Mrs. Meacham's saloon, some of her former confusion rose up. He looked outrageously handsome in his well-fitted jacket and buckskins. His eyes went to her, and she read the admiration there. She didn't bother taking a seat, but just said, "All set?" He rose, made his adieux to Mrs. Meacham, and they left.

"What destination do you have in mind?" she asked.

"I thought we might ride around my land, if that suits you?"

It suited her very well. She was naturally curious to see the extent of his holdings and assumed he was taking her there for that very purpose. As he was accompanied by Cecilia, Sally Gardener didn't think it worth her while to grab a bag and run into the street, but as she already had on her bonnet to do so, she decided to call on the Meachams instead and discover where they were going.

The morning was fair, the heat of the sunshine alleviated by a spring breeze. The couple left the main road as soon as possible and cantered through meadows at a quick pace till they reached Wickham's land.

"I have five thousand acres," he said. "The income is ten thousand a year." This was so pointed she almost felt she should tell him her dowry was thirty thousand, but she refrained, and he continued outlining his holdings. He told her his crops,

130

his livestock, his timber acres, the number of his tenant farmers, and a great deal more about St. Martin's. Cecilia nodded and expressed her pleasure and satisfaction.

"Good company is thin hereabouts," he mentioned. "The Lowreys are connected to me on my mother's side. They live in a large way and are quite sociable. I must take you to meet them one day. Of course, you have your Meacham relations nearby, and there are always friends to entertain from a little farther afield. That, with the London Season, keeps one from being dull."

The more he spoke, the clearer it became that he was outlining the advantages of a match. It could hardly be clearer had he asked her for her father's address to write for permission to offer. As he talked, they continued riding, with Wickham pointing out various features of his estate. When they reached the orchards, he suggested they dismount and walk a little. The rows of trees provided privacy from any prying eyes and lent a romantic aura. Cecilia was as sure she was going to receive an offer as she had ever been of anything in her life. She felt her heart pound as they both looked at the burgeoning apple trees. Buds swelled the branches to pink clouds that had not yet burst. In the treetops, birds warbled their throaty songs.

He would begin by some joking reminder that he was not entirely to be trusted, alone with a pretty lady. His arm would steal around her waist ... Wickham stood some two yards away, and she waited with a palpitating heart for him to come closer. When he came, she just looked at him silently, with glazed eyes. He pulled her into his arms without saying a word. Though surprised, she went willingly enough. His manner was more direct and forceful than she had imagined. This pleased and excited her. When he saw the glitter of excitement in her eyes, his arms tightened, crushing her against his chest.

Her head fell back, and she gazed at his face looming above her. She had thought his expression would be soft, smiling. Its harsh, hungry look astonished her. She even felt a tremble of fear, but before she had time to think or speak, his head lowered and his lips found hers. But when they touched, the kiss was tender, not the predatory sort of attack she had feared. Cecilia tried to keep her head, to assimilate her feelings at being embraced by Wickham.

His lips were warm and intimate. As the kiss continued, she decided she liked the firm warmth of his body against hers. The kiss deepened, and she felt her blood quicken. Her arms tightened insensibly in response to his. Her mind reeled and lost all track of assimilating anything. It wasn't something to be analyzed, but experienced—like falling off a horse, but more pleasant. After a moment she sensed Wickham's attack becoming stronger, and she pulled away.

With a breathless voice she said, "You go very fast, sir."

Now the sweet talk would come. He would apologize for having got carried away. Instead he stepped back, took up a pose, feet splayed, arms crossed over his chest, and an expression on his face that had nothing to do with romance.

"Miss Cummings—Cecilia," he said, "I think you know what all this has been leading up to. I wanted to make sure we should—suit, physically I mean— before speaking. I would be very much flattered if you would marry me." She blinked and looked at him, in his unromantic posture more suited to argument than courting. He was ill at ease. She must cajole him a little, for she had no intention of settling for this cool sort of offer.

"This comes as a great surprise, Wickham. We are only new friends. Why do you offer on such short acquaintance?" A word about "love at first sight" would not have gone amiss—"I knew as soon as I saw you . . ."

"We are well matched as to fortune and social standing, and the other," he added. She blinked in confusion. "Damn, I don't want a wife who flinches ever time I touch her." A memory of Adrianna passed like a shadow over his thoughts. "I need a wife. You need a husband. Elgin and everyone seem to think we would suit. Our interests are not dissimilar. It is true I am a widower, but to counter that, you are no longer quite young."

She felt a strange ringing in her ears. This could not be happening. She was being offered a marriage of convenience! Her dowry was the draw, and her advanced years the price she should pay for his being a widower. Her heart clenched in anger, and two splotches of red formed high on her cheeks.

"You will be surprised to hear I do not consider myself quite reduced to bartering my dowry for a husband yet, sir."

"I did not mean to offend you," he said swiftly, but it was pretty clear that her words had offended him. On top of it all, he had thought she would jump at that insulting offer!

"Did you not?" she demanded, with nostrils flaring. "Can you possibly have thought this offer would be anything *but* an offense?"

"I think we would suit admirably. I have just been telling you how I am situated. You would not find me a demanding sort of husband. Naturally I must have a son and heir—it is the main reason I—"

She had heard enough. "I am in the fortunate position of not having to provide a son and heir, for either myself or anyone else. Without that inducement, I see no reason to marry you, Lord Wickham. I would like to return home now, if you please."

She turned on her heel and went straight to her mare, where she got into the saddle with no help from her escort. He stood gaping, unable to credit her refusal, and the sharp nature of it. When Cecilia dug her heels into the mare and began to clatter away without him, Wickham quickly mounted and finally caught up with her just as she reached the road. Her head was throbbing and unshed tears stung her eyes. Tears more of humiliation and anger than grief. That might come later, but for the moment she was too full of the wicked insult to think of anything else.

Neither one said a word as they raced along the road at a gallop. Cecilia's clenched jaw might have been set in Portland cement, and Wickham hardly looked in a better humor. For a mile they continued in this manner. At that point, an empty hay wain loomed in front of them, taking up the whole road, and they were forced to slow down.

Wickham used the opportunity to try to calm her, for he did not want her running home with some infamous tale. "I'm sorry if you disliked my offer," he said. "It was made in good faith. We are not youngsters playing at romance. You are the one who urged me to marry and pointed out the necessity of providing an heir."

She allowed him one quick, hard glare. "The next time you lumber some lady with an offer, I suggest you at least couch it in less selfish terms. You might at least mention that you admire her."

"I would not offer for a lady I did not like and admire! I had every reason to expect you would welcome my proposal."

"May I know what you mean by that, sir? I have shown you no more than casual politeness."

"I think casual politeness would not have welcomed my embraces." He saw her soaring temper and knew it had been ill-judged to mention that, though it was true. From one folly he hastened into another. "It is the talk of the village that you have set your cap for me. It seems common knowledge that you came to town for no other reason than to make a match. Elgin himself spoke of it quite openly at the abbey."

"Yes, for my *cousins*, not myself. I would hardly leave London, where there are so many parties, if that had been my aim." Cecilia reined in and stopped. Wickham drew alongside her, considering her words, and finding to his chagrin, much reason in them. "What have you heard?" she demanded. "Elgin cannot have led you so far astray as this. He knows my matchmaking proclivities."

"I heard it in the village," he said, flushing at having listened to common gossip.

"I need not ask where!"

"Your behavior seemed to bear out what I heard. You were not opposed to my attentions."

"If you listen to common gossip, you must not expect to be properly informed. Let me tell you, Lord Wickham, my only interest in you was to prevent you from leading my cousins' friends to ruin. For that, I *endured* your company. I begin to think the price paid was too high. Your mount will be returned to the abbey this very day. I do not require your company the rest of the way home."

She turned her mount toward the ditch, took a run and cleared it, and galloped off across a field of rye, heedless of any damage the ride might do. She was beyond rational thought. Her shame was complete, to think the whole village was gossiping about her. It was the last straw when she found Sally Gardener ensconsed in the saloon, with her green eyes staring in curiosity. The only redeeming feature was that the girls were not seated at the window and did not know she had returned alone.

"Why did you not ask Lord Wickham in for a glass of wine, Cecilia?" Mrs. Meacham inquired. She sat with the girls.

Sally could not do without a glance at least of Wickham's back and fled shamelessly to the window. "I do not see him! Did he not accompany you home, Miss Cummings?"

Without thinking, and wanting only to give the girl a setdown, Cecilia replied haughtily, "No, he did not. He was very upset when I refused his offer of marriage and went directly home."

"An offer of marriage!" Sally exclaimed. The others added their wonder to the news.

"Before you broadcast it, Miss Gardener, I ought to inform you I did not accept the offer and would appreciate it if you kept it quiet," Cecilia added. "I cannot imagine where he got the notion I would accept him. No doubt some busybody who knows nothing of me has been whispering misinformation in his ears." With a cold stare at Sally, she turned and swept from the room, to consider her plight in private.

Belowstairs, the wonder and gossip continued. "Why would she refuse him?" Sally demanded.

"I had thought she liked him pretty well," Mrs. Meacham averred. "Such an excellent parti."

Martha had some suspicion that her cousin had fallen under Henley's spell and was foolish enough to mention it.

Alice laughed her to scorn. "If she has a tendre for anyone, it is the man we visited in London, Sir Nigel Pincombe. They seemed very close, and she invited him here for the assembly. Very likely she is planning a match with him, or why else would she refuse such an excellent parti as Lord Wickham?"

Sally demanded an accounting of Sir Nigel and went home with a full budget of news for her mama.

Lord Wickham also pelted home in a temper. He shouldn't have mentioned what Sally Gardener said to him. He already half suspected it wasn't true. What did she know, the simpleton? He shouldn't have made his proposal so abrupt. Miss Cummings was still young enough to want her offer coated in sugar. He should have been satisfied with a simple kiss on the cheek, or at least a light touch of the lips. He had let himself get carried away by those ripe cherry lips. Not the lips of a prude, whatever she said.

By evening he convinced himself he was well out of it. No need to rush into marriage only because Lord Elgin thought it a good idea. Of course he must marry eventually, but not for a decade yet. And never to someone like Cecilia. No, he wanted a plain, older woman, who would be content to tend to her duties and not expect endless love and romance.

Chapter Twelve

Sir Nigel Pincombe and two friends arrived in Laycombe early Saturday afternoon. Cecilia was satisfied that they provided ample competition for Mr. Dallan, who was really the only gentleman still to be brought into line. Mr. Wideman had called the evening before, and while he had not formally asked for Alice's hand, there were enough hints that no fears remained on that score. Sir Nigel was the best of the bucks. She really ought to let Martha have him, but Lord Wickham also required a lesson, and she determined to keep cousin Nigel for her own particular flirt that evening.

Martha could find nothing to admire in any of them. They were tall and handsome to be sure, with each a good fortune, fine jackets on their backs, and more manners and good humor in a finger than Henley had in his whole body, but still they were not Henley. She could not care for the way Mr. Woodhouse laughed, or for Mr. Teale's eyes. They looked sly, as if he were laughing at her. She submitted to going to the assembly in Mr. Teale's carriage, but only if Mama came with her.

This meant Alice and Mr. Woodhouse would go with Cecilia and Sir Nigel. As Cecilia wished a private word with Sir Nigel before the assembly, she suggested they go for a drive that afternoon. They were not long out the door before he said, "What has got you in the hips, Cousin? Are the men proving obstinate? No proposals forthcoming?"

"On the contrary. I have already arranged a match for Kate Daugherty. Alice's beau is nearly there, and I have received a proposal myself. That is what I wish to discuss with you—my own offer."

"Don't have him. He ain't good enough for you" was Sir Nigel's satisfying reply.

"Well, he is, in worldly terms," she said, and outlined Lord Wickham's position.

"I get a sense from your flashing eyes and angry words that something in the offer displeases you."

"It was the manner of it," she confessed, cheeks flaming at the memory. "He as good as called me an old cat. He spoke of the suitability of my fortune, and—oh he was horrid!" Even to Nigel, her bosom beau, she did not go into details as to just how horrid. No mention was made of the infamous embrace.

"But surely you have always said equality of fortune is one of the chief elements. It removes the possibility that one or the other is seeking cream pot love. The man must be a yahoo," Sir Nigel decided.

"Not at all," she defended swiftly. "He is very conversable and intelligent. He is a sort of amateur antiquarian. He had Lord Elgin and some friends at the abbey this week. No, it is not his mind I object to."

"An ugly old wart, is he?"

"Certainly not! He is the most handsome—that is, he is a little something out of the ordinary in that line."

"Clutch-fisted?"

"Oh no, I have no reason to believe that."

"Then it must be his inference that you are no longer seven years old that did the damage. If he is handsome, rich, and intelligent, I see no reason for your refusing him—if you have finally decided to marry, that is."

"I am not one of those ladies who is eager to marry," she said firmly. "I might have had him—in fact, I had pretty well made up my mind to accept him, but the way he phrased his offer! *He* required a mistress for his abbey, *he* required a son and heir, and nothing about what *I* would get from the union."

"Well, you would have got a handle to your name. Countess Wickham. You would get the dignity of being a married lady and the lifetime rights to living in an abbey. What more do ladies ever get?"

"Oh you are so unromantic, Nigel," she said crossly.

"Indeed, I am not! *You* are the one who condemns romance."

"I don't condemn it! I say it is not the *only* thing that matters."

"Youngsters ought not to marry only because they like a man's smile, or his hair or nose or teeth. I have heard you say so times without number."

"I still say it."

"For myself, I plan to fall head over ears in love and make a perfectly shocking match with some beautiful, penniless orphan."

"Now you are teasing," she smiled.

"Well, my dear, I am teasing, but I think I see your problem. You have fallen in love with your Lord Wickham—and he has not fallen in love with

140

you. He only realizes that you would make him a suitable wife."

"I don't know if I love him or hate him," she admitted.

"Aye, but if he came out and said he was mad for you, I fancy we know which it would be, eh?" He observed the flush that bloomed on her cheeks and took her hand. "Poor Cecilia. You can bearlead any gentleman except your own. With all your experience at pulling the wool over gentlemen's eyes, surely you can hoodwink your suitor into thinking he loves you."

"*Thinking* he loves me! *That* is not what I want!"

"You are not using your head, my dear. If you could get him to the altar, he would soon come to appreciate you. Isn't that your theory, that love grows slowly, like a tree?"

"Not that slowly!"

"Well, in my opinion he would do well to get you."

"It is not a question of getting him to the altar, you know. He has already offered," she reminded him.

"Well then, where is the problem? Say yes, and time will do the rest."

"Oh you don't understand," she sighed. "I want—" She came to a wistful stop, hardly knowing what she wanted, or at least ashamed to say it aloud. She wanted Wickham to feel as she felt. She wanted him to speak of love, to kiss her with fiery passion, and tell her he was insanely mad for her.

"You want romance," Sir Nigel said. "I am not a magician. All I can do is help you to make him jealous. I am at your disposal, but pray do not involve me in duels, or anything of that sort. I am a wretched shot and a coward."

"Jealousy has often worked in the past," she said pensively.

"Then we shall be as close as inkleweavers tonight at the dance and see if that don't turn Wickham's eyes green."

"I doubt he will even come to the dance," she said on another long sigh.

In the end, it all depended on Wickham's attending the assembly. On the hope that he would, Cecilia meant to make the best appearance possible and look like a lady worth loving. She wore an ice blue gown she had had made especially for the London Season and had Miser try two new hairdos before she settled on her usual one. The three maidens met in Cecilia's room Saturday evening before going downstairs.

"You must have the first dance with Mr. Teale, Martha. Even if Henley asks you, you shall refuse," Cecilia decreed.

"I doubt Henley will be there for the first dance."

"He will," Alice assured her. "He always comes with George, and George has asked me for the first dance. I may give it to him I hope, Cecilia?"

"Yes, do, but have the second with Mr. Woodhouse and make sure to stand up with him again once during the evening. That will likely be enough to prod George into a proper offer. You might drop a few innocent remarks about Mr. Woodhouse's estate and mention a fondness for his dancing prowess."

"What if Henley doesn't ask me for the first dance?" Martha inquired listlessly.

"Whichever dance he asks you for first, you must

tell him that dance is taken. I shall see that one of our friends stands up with you."

"He may not ask me again," Martha pointed out. "Henley is very proud."

"Yes, unreasonably so, but we shall cut him down to size. Between Alice and myself, we shall let him know Mr. Teale is monstrously fond of you. He will be dangling at your heels all evening."

"What a wretched evening I shall have. I cannot like Mr. Teale's sly eyes, or Woodhouse's laugh."

"There is no accounting for taste. I always prefer a laugh to a sneer," Cecilia said, picking up her pelisse and heading for the door.

They didn't have to pick up Kate that evening. She was being taken by her fiancé. Cecilia wanted to arrive a little late and make a grand entrance with the smart London gentlemen, but the other ladies considered missing a single moment of the evening too high a price to pay, and they arrived on time at the familiar hall, which looked as inelegant as ever. A glance was enough to tell them Dallan and Wideman were already there. They stood with Kate and Andy Sproule, and as soon as the Meacham party arrived, Kate's group headed toward them.

Cecilia made the introductions. She observed with satisfaction the jealous light in Dallan's eyes and felt her little trick was working already. To her dismay, Mr. Dallan hardly glanced at Martha. He bowed to herself and said, "May I have the honor of the first dance, Cecilia?"

"My first dance is taken," Cecilia replied.

Martha looked utterly dazed. She was too capsized to even stick her finger in her mouth, but just stared. She looked ready to bawl. Mr. Dallan then turned to her and said in a perfectly insolent manner, "Then I might as well stand up with you, Martha."

Cecilia was afraid Martha would acquiesce, but anger finally accomplished what common sense could not, and Martha lifted her chin high in the air. "I have promised Mr. Teale the first dance," she replied. Mr. Teale had been well coached. He bounced forward and put a proprietary hand on Martha's elbow.

"Poor luck, old chap," he said to Dallan. "Later, perhaps, if Miss Meacham has a dance free."

Mr. Dallan felt all the shame of being rejected twice in a row. It was only his good opinion of himself that prevented him from making a scene. He gave a careless toss of his head and said to Cecilia, for he would not lower himself to look at Martha, "Rejection, it seems, is the order of the day. First Wickham's offer is turned down flat, now you will not even stand up with me."

Cecilia bristled to hear the news was being bruited about the village. She hadn't even the satisfaction of blaming anyone but herself. She knew it was her ill-advised remark to Sally Gardener that had done the mischief. Certainly Wickham would not have boasted of his rejection.

"The next dance then, Cecilia?" Dallan inquired, trying to look nonchalant, which was difficult when his ears were flaming bright red.

Cecilia felt sorry for him and also wanted a private word to ask him not to broadcast the news of Wickham's offer. "The next dance," she agreed.

Dallan smiled at everyone except Martha and strolled off to the refreshment parlor, where it required three quick glasses of wine to appease his wounded pride. Martha cast a darkly accusing eye on her cousin, but said nothing. Cecilia's first aim, once this little contretemps was over, was to look around for Lord Wickham. She soon realized he was not present, and her heart fell. What a perfectly wretched evening it was going to be! If she got home without coming to cuffs with either Dallan or Martha, she determined she would never try to make a match for anyone again.

The dance with Pincombe gave her an opportunity to calm her nerves and consider what she would say to Dallan. He was bowing in front of her promptly for the next set. She wished it had been anything but a waltz, which left them too much privacy, but a waltz it was. Mr. Dallan held her much too tightly for decorum. She asked him to loosen his arms, which only made him hold her more tightly. She realized he had been drinking more than he should and felt terribly uneasy.

"If we may not embrace in public, then walk outside with me," he said, and gave a leering smile. "My carriage is stabled nearby. Let us go for a moonlight drive."

"You must be mad!" she scoffed.

"Mad with love for you. Marry me, Cecilia. I knew when I heard you had rejected Wickham that you must care for me more than I dared to hope. Why else would you turn down such an offer?"

"I wish you would not speak of that offer. I do not want it broadcast," she said urgently.

"Ho, you might as well ask the wind not to blow. Nothing else is spoken of in town. Wickham was pretty surly about it, when Sally Gardener offered her condolences. I gave him what consolation I could. 'Perhaps Miss Cummings has already committed her heart,' I told him, but till you said yes, I did not tell him I was the fortunate man."

"I have no intention of marrying you, Mr. Dallan. I am shocked that you should have the temerity to offer. I have never given you any indication of interest on my part."

"You have played a sly game, but I see through you," he said, with another leer. "Martha told me of your pains to select my snuffbox. Aphrodite, goddess of love. I read your hint. And in the meadow, when you wanted to be alone to think about us."

Her patience broke. "About us! I assure you, Mr. Dallan, I do not consider that you and I have a single thing in common." She wrenched herself free from his clinging arms and left the floor. Dallan followed at her heels as she went to the refreshment parlor to quiet her nerves. The sight of his inebriated face was more than she could endure. She led him to a corner away from the few couples there and gave him a stiff lecture.

"Let me tell you, I am so far from caring for you that I do not at all approve of Martha's taking an interest in you. She could do much better for herself, and so I have told her and shall continue to tell her. As to marrying you myself, I would as lief marry your groom. You are the most vain, foolish, arrogant, stupid man I have ever met. And now to come to a public assembly inebriated, to make a fool of yourself and me! I suggest you go home and sleep it off, Mr. Dallan. When you wish to apologize, I would prefer that you do it in writing, for I do not wish to meet you in person again, ever."

Mr. Dallan stared at her as if she had struck him. His first flare of anger turned to confusion, then embarrassment, for he had some breeding, hard as he tried to conceal it. "I am sorry if I have offended you, ma'am."

"Well you might be, sir!"

On this she turned and swept from the room before the curious eyes of the onlookers. Dallan realized he was the object of their stares, and felt more foolish then ever. His pride was all that got him out of the room without bawling. He had never felt so humiliated before in his life, and to add to his chagrin, he knew perfectly well he deserved that lecture. But really it was too bad of Martha not to give him the first dance.

He went outside and walked down the High Street, trying to clear his head. What had possessed him to offer for Miss Cummings? In his private thoughts, she was still Miss Cummings. He knew perfectly well she would never have him when she had rejected Wickham. His intention had been to play the heartbroken lover, along with Wickham. He envisaged a month or two of mutual pining over a pint at Jack Duck's. But Wickham had said rather brusquely that he did not plan to frequent Jack's place in future, suggesting that it was beneath a gentleman. There was no point going if Wickham wasn't to be there. And now with Andy engaged and George as well as caught in parson's mousetrap, he would be alone.

The whole village seemed to be mourning for him. Lights were dim in most of the saloon windows, with everyone at the assembly. He stopped in front of Meachams and gazed up at the bow window where he had often sat in former times with Martha, conning the street and quizzing everyone. If Miss Cummings had her way, Martha wouldn't have him. That London swell hanging on to Martha's arm as though he owned her ... Martha, who had never refused him anything before, had refused to stand up with him. Something like panic seized him. He felt a deep urge to hasten back to the assembly—but besides being bosky, he feared what he would do if that popinjay had his arms around Martha.

With nothing else to do, he rode north to Jack Duck's Tavern, to initiate a life of dissolution and heartbreak—then she'd be sorry she had rejected him. Without George and Andy and Wickham, the place was so dreary he hardly wanted to stay. Peg sat with him, trying to cheer him up, so he bought her a bottle of wine. For himself, he ordered brandy, knowing it to be the quickest path to ruin. He had two glasses and went outside to cast up his accounts. After such an ignominious occurrence, there was nothing to do but go home to bed, which he did, with only one detour back to the assembly. He saw through the window that Martha was standing up with another of the London swells. How they loved her! She would cut a wide swath in London society. Would she ever remember him? Would she recognize him ten years hence when she dropped a coin in his beggar's hand? "That looked a little like a gentleman I used to know in Laycombe. I wonder whatever become of Mr. Dallan," she might say to her husband. Cruel world!

Things were hardly more pleasant at the assembly. The draper's wife had overheard an extraordinary thing in the refreshment parlor and took her tale to the most appreciative set of ears in town, the Gardeners'. Before long the story was around that Mr. Dallan had offered for Miss Cummings, and she had treated him shockingly. Henley was a little toplofty to be sure, but to call him stupid and vain was doing it a bit brown. As to saying he was not good enough for Martha, well, they would like to hear Martha's opinion of that!

Sally went whispering in Martha's ear and created as much mischief as even she could desire.

Martha burst into noisy tears and fled to the coat-room, where Sally Gardener was quick to lead Cecilia and stay gaping to overhear the exchange of abuse.

"Why did you tell Henley I would not have him?" Martha demanded through her sobs.

"It wasn't you he was offering for," Sally pointed out helpfully. "It was Miss Cummings herself."

Martha lifted a moist eye from a sodden handkerchief and said in a weak voice, "It cannot be true! You have stolen him from me, Cousin. All your pretense of trying to help me! It was a wicked stunt to steal Henley for yourself. Oh I shall never forgive such treachery. Never! And to think, we invited you into the bosom of our home, never suspecting . . ." She could say no more and gave herself over to uncontrolled tears.

Cecilia leveled a glare on Miss Gardener. "I hope you're satisfied, miss. Pray leave us alone. You will hear no more tales to carry abroad this night."

Sally tossed her curls and hastened off to carry those already heard.

"Martha, control yourself," Cecilia said. "Dallan meant nothing by his offer. He was disguised."

"He wasn't that disguised that he couldn't tell you from me."

"He didn't know what he was saying. He didn't mean it."

"Yes, he did. I knew how it would be. It's not fair, your coming to compete with us. And if you must have a husband, why could you not accept Lord Wickham? I wish you had never come here. I wish you would go home and leave us alone."

Cecilia was still trying vainly to comfort her cousin when Mrs. Meacham came running, alerted

149

to the situation by Sally. Martha threw herself into her mother's arms and begged to be taken home.

"Oh dear, Martha," the mother said, "can you not pull yourself together? Just stay here a spell and have your cry out. There is no saying, Dallan might very well return after he has walked the drink off."

"Yes, return to her!" Martha said, lifting her head and pointing an accusing finger at Cecilia.

"Perhaps we had best all go home," Cecilia said helplessly. "I am truly sorry, Mrs. Meacham. It was none of my doing I promise you. I was as shocked as could be when Dallan blurted out his offer."

"I'm sure you did your best," Mrs. Meacham said, but in no kind way. "This is no reason to drag Alice away, though I doubt she will want to remain with this on our heads. Perhaps you should speak to her. Now hush, Martha. It isn't the end of the world."

Alice was sorry to have to leave such a lively assembly, but could not remain when Martha was in such dire straits. She would go home with the family as soon as she had a word with George.

Staying at the dance was impossible for Cecilia, going home in the carriage with the Meachams equally unpleasant, so she asked Nigel to drive her home. Cecilia heartily wished she had never come to the dance. Her head was throbbing, and on top of it all, Wickham had not even made an appearance. At the door of the house, she begged Sir Nigel to return to the dance and inform her in the morning how much commotion the affair had caused.

"And I'll tell you if Lord Wickham comes, too, and who he stands up with," Sir Nigel added, with a laughing eye. "Are your matchmaking visits always so hectic, Cousin?"

"Indeed no. This one outdoes all the rest. And on

top of it all, Dallan is the most worthless groom I have ever tried to commandeer to the altar. I am not entirely sorry I failed, though it is a pity Martha is so unhappy."

"Perhaps this taste of true love will change your mind about Wickham's offer. A marriage of convenience doesn't seem such a bad thing, eh?"

"It is not love that has caused this brouhaha, but bad manners, including my own. Perhaps I was a little hard on Dallan, but he really is the outside of enough."

"He's a handsome enough devil. I daresay there aren't many to touch him here in the country. At least he seems the sort ladies like."

"Not ladies of common sense. Peagooses is more like it."

She fled into the house and was extremely relieved to see that the ladies had already gone upstairs. Another set-to with Martha was more than she could face. It was obviously impossible to remain at Laycombe. She must leave as soon as possible. As the next day was Sunday, however, there was still one day to be got in. Her thoughts turned to Wickham. One more day when she might possibly see him. She might send a note to the abbey thanking him for the use of the mount . . . But that was paltry behavior, all but begging him to come.

She turned the lamps down low and sat on alone in the semi-darkness of the saloon, looking out at the familiar street, because she could not face her bed. The street looked strangely romantic by moonlight. There half a block down was the shop where she had first met Wickham, and he had picked up the box she dropped. Was that when she first began to fall under his spell? She had been attracted from the first in any case. Love at first sight. How often she had scoffed at the concept.

The simple fact of the matter was she didn't know the first thing about love. How had she passed herself off as an expert all these years? How had she managed to get everyone but herself to the altar with the gentleman of her choice?

It hardly seemed possible that two hours had passed, but when she saw the carriages begin to appear in the High Street, telling the end of the assembly, she knew it must be quite late. Soon Sir Nigel and the others came in. Woodhouse and Teale exchanged only a few words before going upstairs. Nigel stayed behind to give his report.

"Are we utterly disgraced?" Cecilia asked fearfully.

"You were a nine-minute wonder. It ceased to be spoken of as soon as Mrs. Empey caught her feather in the hanging lamp and created a new riot."

"And did—was Lord Wickham . . . ?"

"He arrived just after dinner."

"That's very late! I wonder he came at all. Did he stand up with anyone?"

"Yes, he had a dance with two local girls. Miss Daugherty and a Miss Gardener, who accidentally dropped her shawl in front of him."

"Ah yes, she drops things to great advantage." Neither Kate nor Sally could give her any fear of competition. It looked as if Wickham had gone to the assembly for no other reason but to show he was untouched by her refusal.

The two hour vigil had calmed her nerves, and after a glass of wine with Sir Nigel, she went to bed.

Chapter Thirteen

MARTHA WAS TOO OVERWROUGHT TO GO TO CHURCH on Sunday. Cecilia didn't see her at all, but was told by Alice that her swollen eyes were as red as a ferret's. Mrs. Meacham remained at home to solace her elder daughter. Alice, having left the assembly early, wanted to try for another glimpse of George at church and donned her bonnet to go. Cecilia hadn't the heart to urge Martha out, though it would have done Dallan no harm to see her again with a new beau.

Of the guests, it was only Sir Nigel who was up in time to accompany Cecilia and Alice. Nothing had been said about bringing a guest for lunch, but it was unlikely Mr. Wideman would be turned from the table if he escorted Alice home. Cecilia's main wish was to get herself and her guests out of Meachams' as soon as possible. She knew how unwelcome they were at this troubled time.

They arrived at church early. Alice remained outside chatting to friends, but Cecilia and Pincombe went immediately to the Meacham's pew. With her mind full of her own troubles, she hardly noticed who was attending the service. As the hour for the beginning drew nigh, she glanced at the people flocking into their pews and saw Mr. Dallan. That was a surprise. She made sure he would sleep till noon after last night's dissipation. Some evidence of it still hung about him. His cheeks were pale and his manner subdued. Movement in other seats caught her attention. She saw Wideman was there, and Andy Sproule went to sit with Kate and her mother. Alice came in with them, but darted to her own family pew.

It had not escaped Cecilia's notice that the Wickham pew was empty. A pity Lord Wickham controlled the best seat in the church, since he so seldom occupied it. With a mental sniff she lifted her chin and looked away. Reverend Daugherty was just approaching the altar, and a respectful hush fell over the gathered throng. Into the hush came the measured tread of footsteps approaching unhurriedly. Someone has a good opinion of himself, Cecilia thought. He doesn't hasten his pace when he sees the Vicar is waiting for him. She didn't turn her head to look at the late arriver. It was not necessary. Lord Wickham continued his journey to the front pew where he nodded his thanks to the vicar for his forbearance and sat down.

She felt a jolt on her elbow and looked to see Alice grinning at her, to point out Wickham's presence. That open smile carried a world of meaning. It said Wickham was only here to see her, but Cecilia was undeceived. If she had anything to do with his being here, it was only that he wanted to show her what an excellent, upright fellow she had turned off. She had accused him of leading youngsters astray; he would show her that was not his character. The more likely explanation, however, was that he wanted to listen to the organ again to convince himself it didn't need replacing. All through the service her head was full of worldly thoughts. When she noticed it, she was sorry and tried to pay attention to the service.

Mr. Dallan also found it hard to keep his thoughts on the sermon. What had struck him most forcibly, as he went to his seat, was that Martha had not come to church. Already her smart friends were leading her astray. Having become a heartbroken, unrepentant wastrel himself, he had no right to be there, in God's house, but try telling Mama that! As he had been roused out of a sound sleep and nagged into his Sunday waistcoat, there was nowhere else to go but to church. He had thought he might catch a glimpse of Martha.

Having failed in that, it was his intention to get all the details of the assembly from Wideman as soon as church was over. To this end, he sauntered up to George as he came from the door and asked in a voice of the utmost disinterest, "Anything interesting happen last night at the assembly?"

"Henley, you gudgeon! How did you come to offer for Miss Cummings? You must have been disguised! Martha was a regular waterfall of tears. Her Mama took all the girls home early, and Alice missed half the dance."

"A bit cut up, was she?" Dallan asked, with undiminished boredom.

"Of course she was, and so was I! Why should Alice and I have to miss the dance, only because you were drunk as a Dane?"

Dallan examined his York tan gloves and said, "I meant Martha. Crying a little, did you say?"

"No, she was bawling buckets. If you have any hope of winning her, you'd best get your tail over to her house before she accepts an offer from Mr. Teale in spite."

Dallan looked nobly into the future, which for the moment was concentrated on the old oak tree in front of the church, and said, "A bit late for that, I fear." Then he looked a hopeful question at his friend.

"The sooner you patch it up, Henley, the better. The only other dot of fifteen thousand pounds is Alice's, and I mean to speak to her mama today. Not that the money has anything to do with it. I mean to say—"

"Quite. So you, too, have been caught in parson's mousetrap, George. All the old crowd is breaking up. Andy, you . . ." Noble desolation sat on his brow.

"There's always Sally Gardener. She might have you."

Dallan gave a chilly stare, followed by an incredulous little smile, and left to speak to Wickham. Sally Gardener! Good God, next he would be suggesting Peg, from Jack Duck's Tavern. Fear nibbled at the edges of his mind, but at least he had a noble companion to suffer with.

"Wickham," he said, with a bow. "What brings you to church, you old sinner?"

Wickham nodded. "Dallan. I was surprised you weren't at the assembly last night."

"I didn't hear you were there!"

"I dropped in for a moment."

"Then no doubt you heard of my disgrace."

"I pay no heed to rumors." His eager eye belied this claim. "Some little misunderstanding arose between you and Miss Cummings, I believe?" he prompted.

Aware that there was also difficulty between Wickham and Miss Cummings, Dallan was happy to throw himself into such exalted company. No disgrace in being turned down by her, when she had

156

jilted a lord and owner of an abbey as well. "We were out-maneuvered by the London beaux," he said, with a worldly laugh. "Pincombe, I believe, is Miss Cummings's choice. Sir Nigel Pincombe."

"Is it a serious attachment?" he asked, hiding his concern as well as he could.

"It must be, or she would have had you. I mean to say, Sir Nigel Pincombe, whoever heard of him? But in affairs of the heart, you know, ladies don't know where their best interests lie."

Wickham's eyes traveled across the yards to where Sir Nigel stood with Cecilia. The name Pincombe wasn't familiar to him, but he thought the handsome gallant must be a great favorite in London. "As you say, it must be a long-standing attachment. Miss Cummings could do better, from a worldly point of view."

They were joined by Mr. Wideman. "G'day, Wickham," he said, then turned to Dallan. "Are you coming along to Meachams with us? Alice says she thinks Martha would see you."

"Martha?" Wickham asked in surprise. "I thought it was Miss Cummings you had offered for, Dallan?"

"Oh, as to that," Dallan said, blushing like a green cow, "I was a little disguised, if you want the truth. I always meant to have Martha."

"How very odd that you should offer for her cousin! I never heard you say a kind word about Miss Meacham."

"I didn't really appreciate her till . . ." He frowned, trying to recall just when his love life had gone so wildly astray.

"Till Miss Cummings came," Wideman told him. "It's a great secret. You must not say a word, but I had it of Alice that Miss Cummings came for the express purpose of getting husbands for her cousins. It's a kind of hobby, which is very odd, for she has no interest at all in getting married herself."

"What about Pincombe?" Wickham asked. It didn't occur to him that he was gossiping like a youngster, and was very much interested in what he was hearing, too.

"They are old friends. Well, are you coming or not, Henley? Miss Cummings won't be there. She is dining out with her London friends. Someone invited them all to lunch."

With the last obstacle removed from his path, Dallan said, "If you're sure I wouldn't be imposing."

"Alice told me to ask you."

Dallan glanced along the walk. Alice smiled and waved. It was enough. "I might as well then. We're only having a porker at home."

At the other end of the walk, Alice and Miss Cummings waited on tenterhooks to see the outcome of this meeting. George had hinted that Dallan was ready to repent. Alice had indicated that Martha might be persuaded into forgiveness, and Cecilia had suggested that an invitation be issued to Dallan. Knowing that her own presence might very well keep him away, she invented on the spot a luncheon engagement with friends of Sir Nigel's. All the company from London were immediately invited elsewhere by a fictitious friend.

She waited only to bow civilly to Dallan before leading Sir Nigel off. Alice would be taken home with George. Her eye glanced off Wickham as she nodded at Dallan. As he was gazing at her, she nodded again. He bowed, and left. She and Pincombe made a mad dart to High Street to gather up Woodhouse and Teale and ride into the country to an inn for lunch.

It was a merry meal, with a deal of laughter about Cecilia's idea of entertainment at a country party. "An assembly where the daughter of the house bursts into tears and flies home, and we are hustled out of the house like criminals when company is coming to call. Something quite new in the annals of a house party," Sir Nigel told her.

"I'm sorry, gentlemen, but your presence might have impeded the receiving of an offer of marriage. That is why I was there, you know. Nothing must stand in the way of success."

"Miss Cummings could do better for her cousin than that popinjay, if you want my opinion!" Mr. Teale of the sly blue eyes asserted.

"But she don't want your opinion; no more does Miss Meacham," Sir Nigel told him. "She wants her Mr. Dallan, and no doubt she shall have him. Cousin Cecilia has set her mind on it. God pity the poor gent she decides to have herself. He shan't stand a chance of escaping her clutches." He gave her a conning smile, knowing he was teasing her.

Cecilia laughed as gaily as the rest and kept the irony of it to herself for consideration at a later time and more private place. She kept the company away until after three. By the time they reached High Street, the whole matter was resolved. Mr. Dallan was smiling the warmest, most natural smile Cecilia had ever seen. Martha ran to her cousin and threw her arms around her.

"I don't know how you did it, but you did it, dearest cousin. I hope you will forgive any foolish thing I said last night. Henley was so repentant, so sweet and generous, quite like his old self. It was his falling in with Lord Wickham that did the mischief.

He is well enough in his way, but too high and too fast for Henley. He owns he has been a perfect fool, and that he will never act so badly again. I threatened him I would call on you if he did and that made him look sharp!"

Blaming Wickham for Dallan's folly was bad enough. Being called an ogre herself at the end of all the thanks and praise took some of the pleasure from it, but Cecilia rejoiced for her cousin, and for her own success.

Sunday or not, the London guests realized they were wished at Jericho and bent the travel rules enough to betake themselves to an inn just beyond town for the remainder of the day, whence they would continue to London in the morning. The talk at Meachams was all of weddings and trousseaux and wedding trips. Alice, too, had her offer and thought it would be a novelty for the sisters and their best friend to be all married the same day. Martha wouldn't hear of it. She was the elder; she must go first. Dallan couldn't have his house ready before autumn, and George, whose home was ready for occupancy, couldn't see that he and Alice must wait that long.

Mrs. Meacham was applied to in all the difficulties till her poor head was ringing, and she retired to the bay window with Cecilia, to offer her heartfelt thanks and apologies for any inconvenience to her guests.

"I hope you will stay with us a few weeks till we get the arrangements underway. You see what a mad scramble it will be."

"Unfortunately, I must be getting on to London. The Season is beginning, you know, and Mama will be looking for me. She is in London already."

"But you will return for the wedding at least?"

It was the last thing in the world she wanted. By autumn, however, she thought she might be cured of Wickham and gave a tentative affirmation.

It was a long day, a day of callers and excited conversation and whispered love messages in quiet corners. Dallan found a moment to make an embarrassed apology to Miss Cummings. Cecilia had become Miss Cummings again. "It was the wine speaking," he said earnestly. "I hope you will not think me a fickle fellow. There never was anyone for me but Martha. It is just that I was not used to anyone so sophisticated as yourself, Miss Cummings. You quite turned my head, but I have got it screwed on tight now and know Martha is the one, the only one for me. Your lecture did me a world of good, you know."

She said everything that was proper and did not say, though she felt that he would in all likelihood require another lecture every couple of years. No matter, Martha would have no one but Dallan. As she matured, perhaps she would remember this lesson and know how to handle him.

Cecilia left for London on Monday, late in the morning. While Miss Miser finished her packing, Cecilia sat at the bow window, scanning the street as busily as the Gardeners across the way, but Wickham did not come to town. Her leave-taking was a warm mixture of joy and sadness, with many promises to write, and many reminders that she was to come for the weddings. As the carriage drew away from Laycombe, she tried to project her thoughts into the future.

Usually on her visits, the scene she left behind her faded with the miles, to be replaced by whatever lay ahead. London, or home, or another matchmaking visit. This time, her mind refused to make the change. Her heart, she feared, was left behind. But it was not her heart Lord Wickham wanted. It was her dowry, and her presence as a mistress for the abbey, and her ability to give him a son and heir. It might have grown to love in time ... She would not have spurned such an offer out of hand for any of her protégées. Position was a matter of importance in making a proper match. But no, there must be affection at least—on both sides to begin with.

Chapter Fourteen

BEFORE MANY DAYS PASSED, WICKHAM LEARNED OF the spate of betrothals in Laycombe. Wideman said categorically that Miss Cummings had come as a matchmaker, and as she had left as soon the engagements were arranged, Wickham eventually overcame his pride and believed it. His only informant that Cecilia had come to make a match for herself was Sally Gardener, a tattling gossip whom no one took seriously. What a presumptuous ass Cecilia must have thought him, with his pompous offer. With an acceptance of the true situation came shame and regret. He cringed to think of his behavior.

Why had she not stopped him before the words were out, if she had no interest in marrying him? Why had she let him run on and make a fool of himself? All the time he was riding around his estate with her, outlining his holdings and income—she must have had some idea what he was about. And she had not seemed averse either. She had even allowed him to embrace her. Surely that indicated she meant to accept him? The embrace was as bad as the rest. He had let himself get carried away. One did not embrace an innocent girl as

163

warmly as he had done. Yet the kiss hadn't put her off entirely either. She seemed to like it well enough. He had been certain of acceptance.

An unseasonal spell of raw, wet weather broke out in early May, keeping him much at home, with time to remember and think. She had been ready for his offer—wanted it; why then had she refused? Was it a sudden change of mind? He mentally enumerated his advantages. He was wealthy, titled, popular enough, not without character and address. His person was not unsightly. Was it his former marriage that had put her off? She had known of that before she received his advances.

She had called him selfish. He had made the proposal awkwardly, mentioning only the benefits to himself. Did she expect him to harp on his title and position? He had already showed her around his place. She was well aware of the advantages that accompanied him. Belaboring them would have looked like pride, or worse, bartering. His pride was piqued, but as the days wore on and still the thing festered in him, he realized there was more than wounded pride at stake here.

It wasn't a son and heir he wanted. He was young; there was plenty of time for that. No, it was Cecilia herself, sitting at his piano, her sable curls glinting in the lamplight as she played, that he wanted. It was her bold laughing eyes and insouciant conversation that first beguiled him. It was a lovely woman to come home to, to share his days and nights, his triumphs and sorrows with, that had prompted that offer. It was love, he admitted, and was stunned at his stupidity in not realizing it before. He should have known. He had sworn off love before she came. She was the one who had changed his mind.

He was a hot-blooded man. He would never marry without passion to urge him to it. Since his return, he had spurned a dozen eligible ladies suggested by his relatives as potential wives of convenience. The very idea repulsed him. But Cecilia—without even trying, she had pierced that crust of indifference he had tried to build up after Adrianna's running off . . . But what had Adrianna to do with Cecilia Cummings? They were as opposite as night and day, as frost and fire, as indifference and love. His first marriage was the ill-considered, rash act of a young fool, as unfair to Adrianna as to himself. She could never fit comfortably into his life, but Cecilia would be perfectly at home there. He had not thought of Adrianna's comfort or pleasure. And his second proposal was as bad as his first marriage. He had done it all wrong—because he was selfish. No wonder she had refused him! He was fortunate she had not laid her riding crop across his shoulders.

He was mad, to be suggesting that a young Incomparable with beauty and wealth had come to this backwater to lure him into an offer of marriage, when common sense told him she must be fighting the men off with clubs. The Elgins had said as much. God, what a monster of arrogant stupidity she must have thought him. Eagerness to correct the matter and to show himself in a better light came over him. The miserable weather continued, but it went unnoticed. She might have said yes if he had approached her as a lover. Perhaps it was not too late to undo the damage.

She had been ripe for marriage. When she struck one parti off her list, she would not be long in accepting another. There comes a time in a lady's life when she is ready to settle down, and he feared that time had come for Cecilia Cummings. He had his valet pack his luggage and said he would leave that day.

"Has your lordship forgotten his London house is not open?" his servant inquired.

"Then I'll stay at a hotel till it is."

"You have that meeting with your bailiff tomorrow morning."

"Cancel it, if you please. I'll write him from London."

"May I inquire, your lordship, if something urgent has arisen? Is there an emergency . . ."

"Yes. I must leave at once. Please hurry."

"Then you'll want to notify the Lowreys you won't be dining with them tomorrow."

"I'll send them a note. We'll be leaving in half an hour," Wickham said, with a commanding eye. No further obstacles were thrown in his lordship's path. They left in twenty-four minutes.

Once established in the Pulteney Hotel in London, Wickham was struck with an unaccustomed fit of doubt and indecision. In happier days, Cecilia had given him leave to call in Hanover Square. After what had transpired between them, it seemed like presumption to call. His pride, though more malleable than before, was not so soft as to relish being told that Miss Cummings would not see him. Yet to leave it to chance . . . A week might pass before a casual meeting occurred. Anything could happen in seven days. She had arranged three matches inside of two weeks. How much more speedily might she not arrange one match for herself?

To add to his problems, Wickham had been so long out of the country that he had lost close contact with his former circle. Staying at a hotel made getting in touch with him even more difficult. The Season was just opening, and in the first rush of enthusiasm there were half a dozen parties and routs a night. The ones that he managed invitations to were not those that Cecilia happened to attend. He spent a few days reestablishing his network of friends and relatives, and when his house was open, he had a notice of his arrival printed in the journals.

Cecilia, scanning the social columns daily for just such an announcement, saw it and turned pale. She had heard rumors before, had even thought she spotted him once in Bond Street, but he had not seen her. He had evidently been here for some time, but had not called. There was to be no rapprochement then. She clenched her jaw and told herself it was no more than she expected. Her quick trip to scan the calling cards left on the silver salver in the hall did nothing to cheer her. There was none from Wickham.

Like Wickham, she was sunk to scanning the streets and ballrooms for a glimpse of her quarry. Their first meeting occurred at a small but select rout thrown at Lady Bracken's. Cecilia attended with her cousin, Sir Nigel's, party, as her mother preferred to stay home in the evenings when she could. A quiet musical soiree could always draw her out, or a command to Carleton House from Prinney, but a small rout was not temptation enough to do it. Cecilia stood chatting with friends between sets when she recognized Wickham amidst the throng of black jackets.

Like burning lava upon reaching air, the very sight of him congealed her heat to stone. The only part of her capable of movement was her eyes, that flickered from the proud, dark head, along the half-averted profile of strong nose and jaw, down to his sparkling white cravat. The rest of him was hidden by the crowd. His head turned, and for a moment their eyes met across the room. Both looked away guiltily, as if caught out in a crime, or at least a solecism. Soon their eyes again met, like filings drawn by magnet, and again there was the same swift averting. To an uncertain hope, these quick looks and turnings away were as fatal as being cut dead. Anger was added to hurt and wounded pride in both cases. Cecilia told herself it was for the gentleman to make the first move.

Wickham recognized Sir Nigel as the man who had been at church in Laycombe with Cecilia and felt sure they must have reached an understanding by now. His first instinct to rush off from the scene soon gave way to an unworthy wish to show her how little he was affected. He looked about for the second prettiest lady in the room and secured the hand of Lady Gloria Kirkwell for the next set.

Without once actually looking at each other again over the next hour, each could have described the other's partners to a tee. Cecilia could put a name to the ladies, for she moved much in society and knew everyone. She and Lady Gloria were not bosom beaux, but they had made their debut together five years before, and five years of attending the same parties threw them together often. Wickham only knew that after Pincombe, she had stood up with a sorry looking fellow in a badly cut jacket, and after that with Lord Compeau, who was happily married, and therefore allowed to be not unhandsome in appearance.

After that set, Wickham strolled from the room, not to leave the house, but to fortify himself with a glass of punch. Cecilia caught Sir Nigel's eye and asked him to take her for a glass of wine. She acted from instinct. For years she had been maneuvering gentlemen into marriage, and the first step was always to throw the lady in his path, for little could be done at a distance.

"I see what you are about," Sir Nigel said, as they headed for the refreshment parlor. "I recognized your Laycombe beau. We are following the scent. Which way did he go? We'll run him to ground."

"You are too absurd," she laughed, and tapped his wrist playfully to cover her embarrassment, while hastening to the parlor door.

As they entered, he replied playfully, "No, miss, *you* are absurd, and as transparent as glass. But I forgive you. We should all be absurd when we are in love, or when will we ever be allowed to act the fool without censure? No sane person would willingly shackle himself for life. We have to be fools to marry." He spoke in a teasing manner and in a loudish voice.

Wickham, glancing up, saw them smiling fondly at each other, heard the words "love" and "marry," and turned quickly away to hide his agitation. Cecilia saw him look at her, saw his quick turning away, and was incensed. A demon entered her, and she advanced directly to him.

"Lord Wickham!" she exclaimed, in a pseudo-friendly way. "What a surprise! I had no idea you were in town. Have you been here long?"

"Miss Cummings." He bowed with stiff formality. "I have been here a few days."

"How did you leave all our friends in Laycombe?"

"Tolerably well, I believe. I have not seen them

since—recently, but in a small community, news travels fast."

"You have heard that my cousins are both engaged?" she asked brightly. It was her intention to pretend his offer had never occurred. She would treat him like any casual acquaintance.

"Yes."

His curt reply made conversation difficult, but she forged on a moment longer. "Have you met Sir Nigel Pincombe?"

"I have not had the pleasure."

She introduced them, which did not appear to give Wickham any pleasure whatsoever. "Do you stay in town long, Lord Wickham?" she asked.

"No. That is—perhaps—I have not decided."

"You must not hurry away. The Season is just beginning." Others entered the parlor, and Cecilia, recognizing them, excused herself and went to speak to them. Long practice enabled her to chatter gaily, while her mind was a terrible jumble of confusion.

When she left her friends, she saw that Wickham was gone. "He called his carriage and left," Pincombe told her.

The news struck her like an arrow. She had given him a perfect opportunity to patch up the quarrel. He could have invited her to stand up with him. "Really?" she asked, feigning indifference.

"I expect he has gone on to Saywell's do. I have a card for it . . ."

"No! Let us return to the dance."

Very shortly afterward, she asked Pincombe to take her home. "But as you are interested in going on to Saywell's party, you might tell me tomorrow whether Wickham was there. No, wait!" she said suddenly. "If he sees you there without me, he will know I went home. I would not give him the satisfaction. I can find out from someone else tomorrow whether he was there."

"Am I to be cut off from any further partying tonight?" Pincombe asked. "Really that is a bit heavy, Cousin. I don't mind your using me to make him jealous, but it is the Season. It is only eleven o'clock. I had not planned to retire just yet."

"Could you not go to Brooke's, or one of your clubs?"

"I shall be requiring your services to find me a wife, if I am not allowed to go about and meet the new crop of debs," he scolded, but he agreed that for this one evening he would do as she wished.

Cecilia went to her bed at the unaccustomed hour of half past eleven. She was thoroughly annoyed with Lord Wickham. He had not seemed the least pleased to see her. He would not even have spoken if she hadn't made the first move. Yet he had felt something—there had been an unaccustomed awkwardness about him that did not indicate complete ease. She couldn't take his presence in town as a compliment to herself. He had said he meant to come for the Season. He had not mentioned coming quite so early, however . . .

She had made the first move, and if he didn't follow it up with a call at Hanover Square, she would dismiss him from her thoughts and find herself a different beau. The image in her mind was no longer Wellington against Boney, but the more elementary one of woman versus man.

She learned the next morning where Wickham had gone after leaving Lady Bracken's rout. Sir Nigel called and announced with a laughing eye, "Let me lay your fears and doubts to rest, Cousin. Your

171

Lord Wickham did not hasten along to Saywell's do, to be seduced by Lady Gloria Kirkwell. He went to Brooke's. We had a charming game of faro. It cost me a monkey."

"Did he, indeed, go to Brooke's?" she inquired anxiously. "Then it does not seem he is that eager to find himself a bride."

"He is much more interested in fleecing me of my allowance."

"Did he actually seek you out or did you approach him?"

"He invited me to join him at his table. He seems to prefer my company to yours."

"I daresay he was only trying to discover whether you and I are involved."

"If that was his aim, he's the most desultory questioner I have ever come across. He didn't say a word about you."

She sniffed. "What did he speak of?"

"Cards, horses, the Elgin Marbles."

"Is that all?"

"Certainly not. He asked me to recommend a good barber. Seems a decent sort of fellow."

Cecilia lowered her brow and exclaimed, "If our positions were reversed, Nigel, I would have turned the opportunity to better advantage. I would have said something—"

"What could I say? You want to make him jealous by thinking we are romantically involved, yet to know that you would have him if he were warmer in his advances. That is a hard stunt to pull off. What ought I to have said? 'Miss Cummings and I are thinking of marriage. She is a most charming, lovely, rich girl. You might have her yourself, old chap, if you looked lively.' Tell me what I should have said, and I shall say it next time."

"Oh I'm unreasonable. I know it very well. Are all ladies in love so stupid, I wonder."

"I wouldn't know. None has ever been in love with me."

"I am feeling very dull and blue, Nigel. Take me to Bond Street. I shall buy a new bonnet to cheer myself."

Sir Nigel turned a sapient eye on her. "Yes, he is more likely to be on Bond Street than anywhere else—except perhaps at Somerset House, viewing the Marbles. He spoke of them with some interest."

"I cannot go there. He knows I know he is interested in them. It would look like chasing him."

Pincombe shook his head in wonder. "I had no idea landing a beau was so complicated. They ought to give a course in it at the ladies' seminaries."

"Like university, they only fill our heads with useless stuff and leave us to learn the really useful things on our own."

She got her bonnet and pelisse and they were off to Bond Street. Cecilia bought a charming high-poke bonnet with feather trim and came home uncheered. She had not seen him.

Chapter Fifteen

OVER THE NEXT FEW DAYS, IT BEGAN TO SEEM THAT Lord Wickham had come to London for the purpose of dangling after Sir Nigel Pincombe. As perverse fate would have it, Sir Nigel no sooner delivered Cecilia to Hanover Square with her new bonnet, than he met Wickham at Tattersall's.

"I'm thinking of going to Brooke's later this evening," Wickham said. "Perhaps you would care to join the party, Pincombe?"

Sir Nigel's emotions were mixed. He hadn't the least desire to waste an evening playing cards and losing money, but he felt some wish to help his cousin by becoming better acquainted with her quarry. "Thank you for the kind offer, sir. I cannot afford such costly dissipations, but perhaps we will meet at some do earlier in the evening. Which parties are you attending?"

"None. I've hired a box at Drury Lane. I have not completed my own party yet. Would you care to join me?" While Sir Nigel hastily conned the wisdom of this, Wickham continued, "I have one seat still empty."

One seat was obviously no good to him. If the invitation had been for a couple, he could have

174

asked Cecilia. "I'm afraid that's not possible, Lord Wickham. But again, I thank you for the offer," he said very civilly.

"Another time, then."

"That would be splendid. I look forward to it. I'm promised to Harper's ball, and my friends will want to take in a rout or two first, no doubt. Seatons, and Wiggins—I fancy that is where the younger set will go." There, he had given Wickham Cecilia's complete evening itinerary, and if he hadn't the sense to make use of it—at least the ball after the theater—there was nothing more he could do.

They smiled, they bowed and parted, Sir Nigel flattered at the attention, which really seemed to have nothing to do with Cecilia, and Wickham feeling guilty at this stunt. If he discovered there was an understanding between Cecilia and Sir Nigel, he must desist. But if things were still up in the air, there was nothing ungentlemanly in trying to keep them apart a little. He had carefully planted his box at Drury Lane with Lady Gloria Kirkwell, an exceedingly pretty female friend, in the hope that Pincombe might obligingly tumble into love with her.

Having made his arrangements for the theater, he could not well desert his party and go to the routs instead, but he could drop in for a moment at Harper's ball after and did so.

Cecilia had heard her cousin's account of the chance meeting and knew Wickham would not be free till midnight. Her first chance of seeing him was at Harper's, and till then, the evening dragged abominably. If he didn't come, it was as good as saying he had no wish to see her. But if he came . . .

What she did not take into account was his coming with the rest of his party, including Lady Gloria Kirkwell. Cecilia was so annoyed that she refused to see him at all. Even when he and Lady Gloria joined her set for the quadrille, she hardly acknowledged that he was there. Her smile for Wickham was as chilly as a winter wind, but she was careful to show no spite to Lady Gloria.

To indicate her goodwill in the matter, she stopped after the dance and chatted a moment with the young lady, while Wickham stood beside them, trying to look indifferent. "Have you been in town long, Lady Gloria?" Cecilia inquired.

"We just arrived two days ago. I haven't talked to anyone yet. Who is the best coiffeur this year, and where can I find a decent modiste?"

"You must call tomorrow, and we'll have a good coze," Cecilia said, with a pleasant smile that hid all her jealous anger.

"May I come in the morning? I want to attend to my toilette as soon as possible. All the modistes will be up to their ears in work, and I must get the gown for my own ball started. I got the loveliest new Italian silk at Sanderson's. Everyone is going there this year."

Wickham was allowed to look bored at these female plans, but not to escape unscathed. "Do come in the morning. But your partner is finding our talk tedious," Cecilia said, just flickering a glance in Wickham's direction, without meeting his eyes. "Let us have pity on him and leave our plans for an elegant toilette till tomorrow." She waved her fingers gaily at Lady Gloria and spared a tight little smile for her partner.

"Isn't she pretty," Lady Gloria sighed, as Cecilia hastened away.

"Very pretty. Are she and Pincombe a likely match?" he asked nonchalantly.

Lady Gloria looked dubious. "I really don't know. They have been close friends forever. She seems more attached to him this year than formerly. Perhaps she has decided to have him at last. She could do better from a material point of view, of course. The Duke of Denver was hot after her last year, but she refused him and was seen about town with Pincombe, so perhaps it will come to a match at last."

"Denver!" he exclaimed. "Why would she refuse such an eligible parti?"

"It is a mystery," Lady Gloria confessed. "She makes everyone else get married, but to my certain knowledge, the only gentleman she ever admitted having a tender for was Byron before he turned into a lecher. She must be a deep-dyed romantic at heart. I know she has the greatest aversion to marriages of convenience."

A deep-dyed romantic! And to her he made that wooden offer of a marriage of convenience! The more he heard, the more his heart was beguiled, and the more certain he became that she must despise him. Yet his mood did not turn from desperation to despair. The more desperate he felt, the more determined he became to repeat his offer in more attractive phrases.

Lady Gloria duly called on Miss Cummings the next morning at Hanover Square. Amongst a number of less interesting comments on bonnets and balls and beaux she said with a heavy sigh, "Five years we have been on the town, Miss Cummings. I am determined to make a match this year if I have to marry the rag and bone man."

Cecilia felt a spasm of alarm. "Why I thought you and Wickham were a match. I see you two about everywhere."

"I doubt I stand much chance with him, though I know he wants a wife to give him an heir, and perhaps he will settle for me in the end."

"Would you be satisfied with such a match, practically a marriage of convenience?"

Lady Gloria considered it a moment in silence. "It would be so very convenient that I doubt I would have the fortitude to say no. And one could very easily fall in love with Wickham, of course. Whether the feeling would ever be returned ... However, the Season is young. Have you settled on Sir Nigel?"

"Oh no!" she exclaimed, and immediately regretted it. If Wickham was about to announce a match with Lady Gloria, she did not care much who she married, but she wanted very badly to marry someone. It would be too ignominious to sit on the shelf while he trod the aisle of St. George's in Hanover Square. "Well, to tell the truth, he hasn't asked me. Perhaps I would not say no."

"He is charming. I've always thought so," Lady Gloria said dutifully, but of course Sir Nigel was not so good a catch as Lord Wickham, of St. Martin's Abbey.

The conversation passed on to other matters, and in half an hour Lady Gloria departed with the name of all the top contributors to fashion tucked into her reticule. Cecilia sat on alone, thinking. It seemed that all Wickham wanted was a mother for his son, and Lady Gloria would do as well as Cecilia Cummings. The one grain of good she had discovered was that Wickham was apparently not interested in gaining a mistress, always a matter of concern. It seemed he meant to be faithful to his wife of convenience. His diversions were innocent almost to the point of dullness. And if he meant to be faithful, it would be possible for love to grow. At least he had not positively offered for Lady Gloria, so he was still fair game.

Cecilia pondered ways and means and places of being alone with him. She thought of Elgin's visit to the abbey. Wickham would be calling on the Elgins, probably without Lady Gloria, but when? She could hardly camp out on their doorstep in the hope of encountering him. And he might offer for Lady Gloria at any moment. Her chances for winning him might be limited to days, even hours. She felt a needle of anxiety stab her. She must do something, and quickly, and she hadn't even had the wits to discover where he would be that evening.

She rang for the tray of invitations and rooted eagerly through them, setting a few aside for further consideration. The name Elgin popped out at her from a card, and she lifted it form the stack. It was for a musical soiree, not the sort of place Wickham would take Gloria, but a do he might very well feel obliged to attend himself.

Over luncheon, her mother said, "Where are you off to this evening, my dear?" Mrs. Cummings was an older version of her daughter. From the vivacity of youth she had settled comfortably into her middle years. She liked company, but preferred the less bustling outings than routs now. Music was her particular preoccupation, and as Cecilia was by no means a deb, she did not scruple to let her manage her own private life. Cecilia made a good excuse for her to come to London each season. Her husband preferred staying home with his sheep.

"I thought I might attend Elgin's musical evening with you, Mama. You are going there, I collect?"

Her mother gaped in astonishment. "Indeed I am.

179

You know how I love music. It will be just a small private concert: a piano, a violin, a violoncello, and a tenor. I do not suggest you come. You would despise it, but I hear Signor Bonomi is excellent."

"I should love of all things to hear Bonomi. I shall accompany you."

Her mother shook her head, undeceived by this passion for Bonomi. "Who are you finding a husband for this week, eh? That is what draws you to Elgin's quiet do. I don't know what all the young couples would do without you, but I wish you would find a match for yourself. Five years on the town, and you so pretty. Don't waste your time on the Elgins. Go out and dance and flirt and find yourself a husband. Lady Sommers is calling for me, so you will have the carriage if you need it. Or are you going out with young Nigel?" She knew Nigel to be an old favorite and had some hopes of a match forming.

"I have been using too much of Nigel's time. He will want to be chasing the debs. I shall attend Elgin's soiree."

Her mother sighed in resignation. "Whatever for? There will be nothing there but caps and gray heads."

"I met the Elgins when I was in Laycombe. I—I should like to see them again. Was I included in the invitation?"

"Yes, but I sent in only one acceptance. Not that it will matter, for I am not going for dinner, and another chair can always be squeezed into the music room. We will be three in the carriage, Lady Sommers and myself, so that is no problem. But I cannot imagine that you will enjoy yourself in the least."

"I shall accompany you."

Her mother looked worried at this freakish notion. "I hope you are not thinking of setting up a
flirtation with Bonomi. He is extremely fat, Cecilia."

"It is his voice I am interested in, Mama."

Her mother gave her a knowing look. Tenors indeed! "I see what it is. You are planning to make
some poor unsuspecting lad get married against his
will, and need Lady Elgin's help. Very well then,
you shall come with me."

Cecilia was by no means sure she would find her
quarry there. And if she did not, it would be a dull
scald. The caterwauling of Italian tenors was not
her idea of music to the ears. But if he went, he
would not be likely to have Lady Gloria or any other
young lady with him. He might even suspect that
she would be there. He had attended Harper's ball
after Nigel told him she was going.

She wore the satin gown with rose lace overskirt
she had worn to the first assembly in Laycombe,
hoping to stir memories in Wickham's heart. He
had flirted outrageously with her that evening. He
had not spoken of dowries and heirs on that occasion. How did it come that he had flirted when he
was not serious, and turned into a block of wood
when he proposed? Her coiffure was arranged in
the same tousled manner as before, with the little
diamond star over the ear. She wore the same white
kid gloves, and carried the same fan. Outside, she
looked the same, but how her heart had changed.

The change was reflected in the feverish glitter
of her eyes, and the warm flush of her cheeks as
she entered the Elgin mansion. Her first object was
to discover whether Wickham was there. Her eyes
scouted the entrance hall in vain. Perhaps he was
in the music room already. She would nip in while

Mama spoke to Lady Elgin. If Wickham sat alone, she would sit beside him to exchange a few words. "What a surprise to see you here, Lord Wickham! I had no idea you were interested in singing."

The words were never spoken. Wickham was not there, nor did he come during the extremely aggravating hour of Italian caterwauling. For sixty minutes she sat forlornly, imagining him out waltzing with the beautiful Lady Gloria, perhaps even this instant making his offer. By the intermission, her head ached wretchedly, but she forced a smile and went out with her mother for a glass of wine. Every fiber of her being was on thorns to escape, to dart off to a more interesting party where she might run across Wickham. She could not ask Mrs. Sommers to oblige her, so she glanced around the throng for someone else who might be planning to skip the second half of the concert.

Her eyes peeled over all the caps and gray and bald heads in the refreshment parlor. A younger man or couple was what she required. Her eyes were drawn by a sandy-haired gentleman just slipping inobtrusively from the crowd. It was Mr. Larraby. He was an old friend, no real lover of music but a connection of Lord Elgin who had come to flatter him into writing an article for his journal.

"Mr. Larraby," she smiled. "I see you drifting toward the door. Is it possible I am in luck, and you are about to shab off from this dull do?"

"You've caught me dead to rights," he admitted, "but no need to announce it. I have made an appearance. That's enough to establish my good intentions. I am off to livelier dissipations. Can I give you a lift home?"

Home was no good. Although no longer a deb,

Cecilia was not yet ancient enough to attend the balls alone. "Where are you going?" she asked.

"I promised the Millars I would look in on their party."

This would be an unexceptionable do, and if Wickham was not there, she could latch on to another party and continue her hunt with other friends. "Would you mind taking me with you?"

"I would be honored!" he answered readily.

"I'll just tell Mama and get my pelisse."

Within two minutes she rejoined him in the hallway. The crowd was just beginning to return to the music room, and they hastened to the front door to escape unnoticed. The butler was already at the door, drawing it open. As Cecilia stepped out, Lord Wickham was just entering.

"Cecilia!" he exclaimed. Shock at seeing her made him forget the new formality between them, and he addressed her in person as he did in his thoughts. For a brief moment their eyes met, before darting away. The look, though brief, was extremely conscious. He looked as if he had been caught out in some petty crime, and she feared she looked the same way, for it was exactly how she felt.

"Not leaving so soon!" he said. He glanced at Mr. Larraby, holding on to her elbow, and noticed the change of escort. That was a good omen at least. It seemed she was not completely in Pincombe's pocket.

Cecilia had to swallow all her chagrin. Frustration lent an angry tinge to her voice. "As you see, but if you hurry, you can catch the last half of the concert."

Caught off guard, Wickham stuttered and stammered, trying to discover where she was going and to extricate himself from the boring concert. He had only come in desperation as he could not find her anywhere else. "I am not really that fond of Italian singers. I came from a sense of obligation to Elgin."

"We are all in the same boat," Mr. Larraby laughed. "I am here to twist Elgin's arm to do me a favor, and Miss Cummings—why to tell the truth, I cannot imagine why you are here, ma'am." He looked a question at her.

Cecilia found both gentlemen waiting for her answer. She cared very little what Mr. Larraby might think; her concern was all for Wickham, and it was at him that she looked. In a flash it occurred to her that Mr. Larraby had just revealed that he was not really her partner, or he would know why she was here. It was as good as telling Wickham that she was chasing him. In a bustle of confusion she said, "I was obliged to accompany Mama, but my duty is done now, and I am off to meet Sir Nigel at Millars." She looked to see if Wickham had any thought of accompanying them. His penetrating stare told her nothing.

"I highly recommend it," he said. "I have just come from there. A very lively party."

"I wonder that you chose to leave it so early," she said. It struck an echo from the past. She had said something similar to him in Laycombe.

"It is more a matter of duty than choice. I promised Lady Elgin I would drop in."

"Then you'd best hurry, Lord Wickham. The audience is rushing for the seats now. Nice meeting you again."

Wickham could find no excuse to linger. He bowed and passed on into the house as Cecilia and her escort left. Mr. Larraby found her a very indifferent companion that evening. She hardly said a word as the carriage took them to Millars. Once she said, "I believe I shall just go home, after all, Mr. Larraby, if you don't—" Then she stopped. But Wickham might return to Millars. The rout would last longer than the concert. "No, Hanover Square is out of your way."

"I don't mind the detour, if you would like to go home," he said promptly.

"No, no. We shall go to Millars." Very likely Nigel would be there.

Lady Elgin saw Wickham entering and had a word with him. He slipped into the back row as the audience was already seated. His mood was not so obvious as Cecilia's. His look of concentration as he sat in the music room, ears deaf to the racket, might be mistaken for appreciation of the performers. He sat through two numbers, during which he discreetly drew out his watch three times. At the end of the second selection it was eleven-thirty, and he felt as if he had been locked up for an eternity. She was at Millars. It almost seemed she had made a point of telling him where she was going, though he disliked that mention of Pincombe. He had told her this was only a duty call. She would not be surprised if he returned to the rout. He rose and slipped quietly out of the room.

Within twenty minutes he was back at Millars's rout, searching the hall for Cecilia. She was performing a country dance with Pincombe. She had arranged to meet him here then. His heart was heavy as he watched her from an inconspicuous corner, admiring her trim figure, deeply resenting the black arm around her slender waist. He did not notice that she wore the same gown she had worn at Laycombe. His attention was more closely riveted on her face. How lively and vivacious it was. Five minutes before it had been a perfect mask, but she had seen him and was now not only vivacious, but in a panic of pleasurable alarm.

As the dance ended, Lady Gloria spotted Wickham and came forward to welcome him. "I thought you had left, Wickham!"

He bowed politely and tried to look happy to see her. "I had a duty call to make at Elgins." She looked as if some further explanation was necessary and he added, "I could not like to drag you away from the ball for such a dull do."

"I have the next dance free," she said hopefully.

"That is fortune rewarding me for having done my duty. May I have the pleasure, Lady Gloria?"

Indeed he may. It was a set of waltzes, and while he waltzed with Lady Gloria, his eyes sought out Cecilia. She was standing up with Pincombe again. Two sets in a row looked as if they were serious, perhaps even betrothed. Miss Cummings was too polished not to realize the significance of honoring one partner so strongly. He felt his suit was hopeless. He wouldn't accost her. Yet when the music ended, they stood close together, either by chance or by planned arrangement on someone's part.

Pincombe made the first move. "I see you returned, Lord Wickham."

"Yes," he said, and felt embarrassed, lest Cecilia suspected his reason. Pride disdained admitting he was in love with her unless the emotion was returned. "I had to leave briefly, but hurried back." A smile in Lady Gloria's direction hinted she was the reason for it.

Cecilia felt a lava rush of jealousy and spoke without thinking. "Ah we understand how it is, do we not, Nigel?" Her stormy gray eyes turned lovingly to her cousin.

Wickham's reaction was more violent than she expected. He gave a jolt and exclaimed, "Are you engaged then?"

Nigel looked to her for a reply, and in the *gêne* of the moment, they both emitted a nervous laugh.

"Oh you *are*!" Lady Gloria exclaimed. "How wonderful. I always felt you two suited so very well. Congratulations, Sir Nigel. And Miss Cummings, you sly boots. Not a word of this did you mention this morning."

"We were not engaged this morning! That is—we are not exactly—"

Nigel saw her floundering and leapt to her rescue. "We haven't announced it yet. Mum's the word. Till our parents know what we are about . . . ."

"Of course," Lady Gloria smiled forgivingly. "I shan't say a word, but I want to wish you both happy."

"Thank you," Cecilia said, and grabbed Nigel's arm to escape at top speed. "Why did you say that?" she demanded, the moment they reached the door.

"I had to say something. You were gasping like a fish out of water. Good God, what are we to do now? There is no counting on Lady Gloria's discretion."

"She said she wouldn't tell."

"I'm pretty sure Lady Jersey overheard, and if Lady Gloria doesn't tell the world, you may be sure Silence Jersey will."

"Oh dear, what can we do?"

Sir Nigel pulled at his earlobe and said, "I expect we'll just have to get married."

Chapter Sixteen

LADY GLORIA KIRKWELL CAME WITHIN AME'S ACE OF receiving an offer of marriage from Lord Wickham. If she had accepted his stilted offer of a drive home with him, delivered before the next set of dances began, she would have had it that very evening while his temper was at its peak. His expression looked so far from romantical that she decided he had a megrim and saw no reason why she should cut short the ball, only to oblige him. She had half a dozen other beaux in her eye as well as Wickham. So Wickham went to Brooke's Club instead, to vent his ill humor on a game of faro. In a pitch black mood, he almost wanted to lose his fortune.

Cecilia's evening ended a little less foolishly. She had Nigel drive her home directly and made him go into the house with her to discuss their situation. "Do you think he loves her, Nigel?" she asked, when they were ensconced on the sofa with a glass of wine.

Sir Nigel considered it a moment. "I shouldn't think so. He leapt like a shot rabbit when he asked if you were engaged. Why would he do that if he was in love with Lady Gloria?"

"That is my own feeling," she confessed. "I think

he loves me and doesn't know it. I cannot like to see him—and Gloria—marry under such inauspicious circumstances." She gave her cousin an uncertain look. "I daresay he would not like to see me make a bad match either."

"Yes, it's a pity I'm such an unexceptionable gentleman," Nigel grinned. "If I was a rake or fortune hunter or serious toper, I daresay he would dislike our match as much as you dislike his."

"I expect he might even do something to hamper it," she said, glinting a meaningful look at him.

Nigel suspected that look. He had seen it before when Cecilia made him lend her a set of trousers and man's jacket to sneak into the cockfighting barn in disguise. He had seen it when she made him give her an alibi while she went to the Pantheon masquerade. He had seen it dozens of times, and it always spelled trouble for him. "No!" he exclaimed, on general principle.

"You haven't even heard my idea yet!"

"The answer is still no."

She sat down, let her head droop wearily on her chest and drew a deep sigh. "Very well, Nigel. I cannot expect you to put yourself out when it is only my life's happiness that is at stake," she said, with suspicious docility. "What is that to you? I daresay I would be equally disobliging were the situation reversed. I did not mind telling your papa it was my idea when you borrowed his hunter to race Teale, but of course that was years ago, when we were young. It is true I have done you a few favors since then," she added, hitting him with an accusing eye, "but I do not blame you for abandoning me now."

He knew he would help her in the end, and said,

"Cut line, Cecilia. I know I owe you a few favors. What is it you have in mind?"

She glanced up at him uncertainly. "I only want to give Wickham the notion that you are—unsteady in character."

"Oh lord! I suppose it is to be bruited about town that my pockets are to let."

"No, I shouldn't think that would do it. He knows I have thirty thousand. It must be something serious."

"Good God! My blood runs cold to think what you have in mind if being a wastrel is not serious."

"It is not so very bad after all."

"No, nothing at all. I am only to be a monster of some sort of dissipation. What is it to be—drink, women, cheating at cards?"

All these had occurred to her, only to be discarded. "No indeed, I could not like to blacken your character. I want you to become a monster of rectitude. You must hint to Wickham that once we are shackled, you mean to bounce me off to the country, to raise your children and hold house while you continue racketing about town. I expect it is more or less what he had in mind himself," she added, with an angry twitch of her shawl.

"Then he will not see much amiss in it, will he?"

She gave a sly smile. "Oh I think he will. He realizes now that such a life would not suit me. And I think—I do hope I am not wrong—that he loves me. That must make a difference, Nigel."

Nigel was not perfectly satisfied with this plan, but as it was so much less horrendous than he feared, he was willing to go along with it. None of his friends would believe such a faradiddle, so the story could not do him any irreparable harm if it got loose. "When am I to display myself to Wickham in this draconian character?"

"The sooner, the better."

Sir Nigel rose and said, "Why waste a moment? I expect he is at Brooke's by now, waiting to fleece me of what few shekels I have left. Brooke's is where he goes to drown his sorrows."

"Then you must go at once. Call on me tomorrow morning and let me know. Either way, whether he is there or not, call on me. And Nigel," she added, "you may tell him I have not positively accepted your offer—if he happens to inquire, I mean."

"Hussy!" he said approvingly. Sir Nigel bowed and left. He intended to do more than Cecilia had suggested. Her romance with Wickham was taking up too much of his time. He wanted to have it settled before he wasted the entire season. When he reached Brooke's, Wickham was there, but not ensconced at a gaming table. He stood on the side, drinking brandy and looking as glum as he felt, while waiting to join a game. He didn't approach Pincombe on this occasion, so Pincombe got a glass of wine and went to him.

"Ah, Wickham," he smiled. "You are like me. Do the pretty with the ladies early in the evening and peel off to enjoy the best part of the night without them."

Wickham's black brow rose. "An odd point of view for a man who has just become engaged, Pincombe."

"Ha-ha, as to that, the lady has not positively accepted me."

"Indeed!"

"She is considering my offer. To tell the truth, I am not sure I have chosen wisely." Wickham looked interested, and he continued. "The thing is, I fear

Miss Cummings has some odd notions of a lady's matrimonial duties. She stiffened like a starched cravat when I mentioned how we would go on, after the wedding."

"Do you harbor some unusual views on holding house?"

"Not in the least. I hold that a wife's place is in the home, the country seat, I mean. A fellow cannot like to leave his estate untended while he is in town on business. Someone must keep an eye on the servants and the kiddies. I don't approve of couples having their Season in town after they are married. The wives ought to stay home. They only get into mischief if you let them loose in town. There are too many fellows wanting to take advantage of them."

This was a subject close to Wickham's heart, after his experience with Adrianna. "You are half right," he said, "but there are other ways of avoiding that mischief. Both stay at home or go out together."

"What—a man and wife to be harnessed at the neck like a pair of oxen? Not the thing, old chap. I mean to say—why bother coming to town if you are only going to squire your own wife, eh?" A lascivious smile accompanied this remark.

"Miss Cummings was averse to your ideas, you say?" Wickham asked, with an air of indifference.

"She was stiff, Lord Wickham. Stiff. I thought it only fair to give her a hint how we would go on in the future, for everyone knows Miss Cummings enjoys her Seasons. I daresay I can talk her around. She is not quite an ape leader, but she has hung on the family tree a few years, what? She will be happy enough to settle, I think."

Wickham called for a bottle of brandy and joined

Pincombe at a table to give him a thorough quizzing on this interesting matter. When Pincombe's head began to reel from the unaccustomed brandy and when he felt he had done as Cecilia wished, he rose to leave.

"Are you seeing Miss Cummings tomorrow?" Wickham asked.

"Aye, I'm taking her for a drive in the afternoon. She can't get into much mischief in a carriage. I mean to get an answer from her, one way or the other. And if she refuses, Wickham—I was just wondering whether you and Lady Gloria—I mean has she accepted you?" Cecilia would be interested to know this.

"I have not offered for Lady Gloria."

"She has only ten thousand pounds, of course. But she seems a biddable sort of lady. Hmmm."

"I doubt you will find any lady in this day and age as biddable as you require, Pincombe." He wanted to see them together, to see how Cecilia reacted to her new suitor. He also wanted that occasion to hold an opportunity for some private conversation with Cecilia. "I expect you'll be attending Kirkwell's rout party tomorrow evening?"

"By jove, yes. That is, I haven't discussed it with Miss Cummings, but I shall certainly be there. Especially if Miss Cummings give me my congé. Only ten thousand dowry—but a very biddable girl, Lady Gloria, and well connected."

They parted, Pincombe to go to another club for supper, Wickham to nurse his drink and consider their conversation. Pincombe seemed to have changed his stripes overnight. He had not worn this hypocritical face before. Wickham suspected a plot, but there was enough possibility of truth in what he had heard that he wanted to warn Cecilia what

193

she was falling into. It did not escape his memory that she had very roundly rejected his own offer. It had been bad, but not so bad as this.

Pincombe called on Cecilia the next morning and described the meeting at Brooke's. "I hope you didn't overdo it!" was her main worry.

"I was as smooth as silk. And I went beyond your instructions, too."

"Oh dear!"

"You ain't the only one who can scheme and make matches. I may set up as the new matchmaker when you hang up your—er—title? I only asked him if he had offered for Lady Gloria. He hasn't, but he is attending her mama's rout tonight. I told him we would be there and laid the groundwork to detach her from him, if that is what you require."

"I have not yet decided what I require," she said pensively. "But call for me this evening. I'll know by then."

By evening, Cecilia had decided she would be more docile to Pincombe's specious demands than her true nature would warrant, but not such a doormat as to be incredible. She would allow herself to chafe at the bit, without bolting. With Miss Miser's assistance, she made an impressive toilette, featuring not her diamonds but a small set of emeralds, that set off her Italian *peau de soie* gown very effectively.

Her heart was in her throat as she and Pincombe stood on the landing at Kirkwell's rout, surveying the crowd below. Wickham was there before them, not dancing, but just standing on the side. She saw him detach himself from the wall and advance to the bottom of the stairs to meet them. He felt a sense of urgency, then . . .

194

She curtsied gracefully. Wickham bowed, and they exchanged a few social nothings till the quadrille began. She stood up with Pincombe, and at the dance's end they met Wickham again. He had stood up with Lady Gloria and made a dash to intercept them. "Hot work, dancing. Shall we go for a glass of wine?" he suggested.

"An excellent idea," Pincombe replied. Then he turned aside to Cecilia and said, "Just one glass for you, mind. I have noticed you are drinking a little more than you used to, Cecilia."

Cecilia laughed. "One would take you for a Methodist, Nigel."

"You are mistaken. A Methodist would not allow you even one. In fact, he would not be at a dance at all, unless he came with a constable to bar the door. There is something to be said for Methodism."

The group went together to the refreshment parlor. "I didn't see you at the park today, Miss Cummings," Lady Gloria mentioned.

Pincombe answered again, assuming that in the normal way this would annoy Cecilia. "Miss Cummings had to do a little errand for my aunt," he explained. "We had planned to drive out together, but my old Aunt Lavinia Dicaire needed some work done on her diamond bracelet. I asked Miss Cummings to attend to it, as I had to see my barber."

Wickham looked to see how Miss Cummings liked being used as an errand boy. She smiled demurely and said nothing about it. "This is a lovely rout, Lady Gloria" was her comment.

"Enjoy it, my dear," Pincombe said, with a doting smile. "You must get your fill of waltzing, for next year you will have weightier matters to fill your time. I should like to have at least one crib in my nursery filled by next year."

Cecilia allowed a little chill to creep into her tone. "I would remind you of that old saw about not counting your chickens, Nigel."

He laughed good-naturedly. "You've danced enough years, my dear. It is time you learned to enjoy the comforts of domesticity."

"I am not tired of dancing yet," she said saucily.

"Then I shall ask Lord Wickham to give you the next set. You will be safe from harm with Lord Wickham." He turned to Lady Gloria and sought her company. Sensing that Cecilia desired privacy with her victim, he took Lady Gloria's arm and led her away.

Wickham surveyed Cecilia through narrowed eyes, looking for signs of that quick temper that he knew her to possess. She smiled docilely. "It was presumptuous of Sir Nigel to assume your complaisance in standing up with me, Wickham," she said.

"I should have said the fault was in his choosing your partner for you, ma'am," he parried.

"It is his notion of protecting me. He seems a trifle high-handed to be sure, but he means no harm."

"I had not thought you were a lady who required that degree of protection."

"You are referring to my vast, though vicarious experience in the marital arena, I collect? You need not fear for me, Wickham. If I find something I dislike in my husband, I shall change it."

"That is easier done before the wedding, ma'am."

She gave him a saucy look. "But then one runs the risk of frightening the prey away."

"You are referring to my wretched performance at Laycombe," he said, with a touch of embarrassment.

"That was unworthy of me, but it was my meaning, I confess."

"You must feel a strong attraction to Pincombe, as you are willing to accept from him what you refused in me."

Cecilia allowed a troubled frown to pleat her white brow. "Perhaps you were right after all. There is much to be said for a marriage of convenience. I daresay all marriages sink to that in the end. It is just that one could wish to see them at least begin on a more romantic note," she said wistfully.

She felt the very air palpitate with his disagreement, knew he wanted to contradict her, and knew as well that the refreshment parlor was too public a spot for any powerful show of emotion. "We had best go back to the hall," she said, and gave another wistful smile. In her eyes was reflected a nostalgic memory of his offer and even something for her regret at having refused it, as she was sunk to a marriage of convenience in the end. If he had an atom of gallantry, he would find a way to reclaim her.

"I see no reason why romance should be limited to the beginning," he said, and placed her hand on his elbow. They strolled slowly from the parlor out into the hallway. Across the hall a door showed them a small, private room. It looked like a ladies sitting room. There were comfortable chairs before the fire and two workbaskets on a table. "The music has not yet begun yet," Wickham said. "May I talk to you for a moment, Miss—Cecilia?" His voice softened as he spoke.

"For a moment," she agreed, in a breathless voice.

When they were alone, the mood was uncomfortable. Wickham knew it was abominable for him to proceed with his own offer when she had given every indication of accepting Pincombe's. She knew he knew it and feared he would let gentlemanly scruples stand in the way of their happiness. Being no gentleman herself, she knew the first move was up to her.

"Oh what should I do, Wickham?" she asked helplessly.

"If your mind is quite made up, I cannot attempt to dissuade you," he said through clenched lips, but he looked very much as if he wanted to dissuade her.

She made a pretty moue and tossed her head. "It is not made up," she said crossly. "I would not ask for advice if I had already decided. But I have chosen my confidant poorly. You, I know, are not against marriages of convenience."

It was enough. All his anger and frustration came blurting out. "I loathe and despise them! You should box Pincombe's ears and send him packing. I cannot imagine what you are about, to smile and smirk at that puppy's insolence! Limiting you to one glass of wine and telling you who to dance with. To speak of you as though you were some weary drudge who should submit to becoming a brood mare for him."

"He hasn't suggested anything different from what you said, or at least meant, when you made me an offer."

"To my shame. But your good sense treated that offer as it deserved. Good God! I had more respect for you when you combed my hair with your riding crop!" he said belligerently. His color was high, and anger flashed in his dark eyes. "What has changed your mind? What has changed *you*?"

His anger acted as a catalyst to hers, and she shot back, "Age and experience have changed me, sir. I see that all men are alike. Arrogant, overbearing, selfish, stupid—beasts!"

His complexion heightened from pink to red. "Then why are you marrying him?" he demanded.

"I haven't said I am. And in any case, he is no worse than the rest."

"Do you love him? It must be love. Nothing else could make you behave so foolishly." His eyes, staring into hers, looked impenetrable, but on the surface she read the gleam of fear and was hopeful.

"No, I don't," she said softly.

"Then why? If you only want a husband, *any* husband, have me. I offered first." He grabbed her hands and spoke ardently. "Cecilia, I was an idiot. I didn't know what I was saying. I had decided to marry; you were there—I spoke on the impulse of the moment, thinking and saying only what was to the advantage of myself. I married for love once—it was a disaster. But that wasn't love's fault. It was an ill-advised match from every point of view. I knew we would suit better. My pride was wounded when you refused, but I soon learned the greater blow was to my heart. I felt desolate without you. I came scrambling to London for the sole purpose of apologizing, of telling you I love you."

The color drained from her face, leaving her pale and giddy with happiness. "Oh! But why didn't you *do* it?"

His hands slid up her arms, drawing her close. "Because I thought you must despise me. I had to soften your anger first."

"And set about it by courting Lady Gloria!"

"I wasn't courting her! You were running about everywhere with that jackanapes of a Pincombe. He had already come bounding down to Laycombe after you. I was afraid the matter was all arranged." His arms went around her, and she laid her head against his shoulder.

"You wrong Nigel. He was of great use to me," she said softly in his ear.

He lifted her head and saw the laughter glinting in her gray eyes. A reluctant smile softened his harsh expression to tenderness. "Cecilia Cummings, you are a born schemer! I half suspected last night when he came ranting at me like something out of the last century. You put him up to it!"

A throaty gurgle of laughter issued from her cherry lips. "I had to do something. You were so slow in taking all the leads I tried to give you."

"You'll have to marry me. It isn't safe to leave you loose on the town, coercing innocent fools into marriage. My mind is already made up. You can do me no harm."

"Can I not, Wickham?" she taunted, and was kissed soundly for her impertinence. The kiss was no gentler than the first one received in his meadow. The same strange swelling inside occurred, till she feared she would burst. His lips clung hungrily to hers, till at last she pulled back. It seemed wise to set out her terms before she was entirely senseless.

"I want it fully understood that I am not to be sequestered at St. Martin's while you gallivant the Season away without me," she said, with trembling breath.

It was Wickham who noticed the door was open and went to close it. He led her to a sofa before the grate and sat beside her, pulling her head to his shoulder. She lifted it and gazed at him. "Whither thou goest, Wickham," she warned.

He gazed into her eyes. "The Adriatic is just that shade when the sky is stormy," he said dreamily.

"If I happen to be increasing next spring, I shall expect you to stand by me."

His hand caressed her cheek, then rose to ruffle her hair. "Like black silk," he said, rolling a curl around his fingers.

"As to my fortune, it will be entailed on my—our son, in case anything should happen to me, and the use of it will be my own in the meanwhile."

"I was used to think you had a perfectly English face, but I see something Gallic in your smile," he mused.

"It is best to get all the details hammered out beforehand, you know." She realized he was paying not the least attention and said, "And of course I shall want a cicebeo, to be in style in London."

Wickham gave a knowing smile. "You will not be abandoned at St. Martin's, whether you are increasing or no. What you do with your fortune is your own affair, but as to a cicebeo—not while I have life and breath in me, madame. No one will have the opportunity to do—*this* but me." He pulled her into his arms and kissed her passionately.

In Laycombe, Mrs. Meacham received her mail with no particular interest, till she recognized Cousin Cecilia's writing. Then she tore the letter open eagerly and glanced through it. "Why, Cousin Cecilia is getting married!" she exclaimed.

Martha removed her finger from her mouth and said, "Who is she marrying, Mama?" She had won her beau and could revert to all her bad habits.

"Lord Wickham! Can you beat that? I always

suspected there was a little something between them." She rose and hastened from the room.

"Where are you going, Mama?" Alice asked.

"Over to tell the Gardeners," she crowed, and emitted a most unladylike cackle of laughter.

Regency presents the popular and prolific . . .
JOAN SMITH